'Is there room in your life for anyone else to love you?'

Ryan knew he was moving too fast but he had to know. If she said no without hesitation then he might as well give up. Tara could be stubborn, and if she made up her mind about something it was extremely difficult to change it.

But she hadn't answered.

Her cheeks were pink and she was looking at a point somewhere on the opposite wall. He moved a little closer to her and grasped her hand.

She refocused and mesmerised him with her deep grey-blue eyes. Was it desire he saw in their depths?

'You mean you?' she finally said.

'Yes.'

Tara leaned across, rested her head on Ryan's shoulder and sighed.

'Oh, Ryan. Why did you have to come back? I had my future mapped out. I thought I was as happy as I could be. And I honestly can't think of love. Not now. It's too hard.'

Ryan gently stroked her silky hair and resisted the temptation to put words into her mouth. *She* had to say it.

He waited…

Originally a city girl, **Leonie Knight** grew up in Perth, Western Australia. Several years ago, with her husband, two young sons and their Golden Retriever, she moved south to a small rural acreage located midway between dazzling white beaches and the magnificent jarrah forest of the Darling Scarp. Once her boys grew up and left home, and the demands of her day job lessened, she found she had more time to devote to the things she loved— gardening, walking, cycling, reading and, of course, writing. She spent most of her adult life working in first a suburban and then a rural general medical practice. That combined with the inspiration she got from her real-life hero led her to writing Medical romances and to realize her dream of being a published author. Sadly Leonie passed away in 2011. *The Doctor, His Daughter and Me* is her third and final story.

Recent titles by the same author:

HOW TO SAVE A MARRIAGE IN A MILLION
SUDDENLY SINGLE SOPHIE

THE DOCTOR, HIS DAUGHTER AND ME

BY
LEONIE KNIGHT

All the characters in this book have no existence outside
the imagination of the author, and have no relation
whatsoever to anyone bearing the same name or names.
They are not even distantly inspired by any individual
known or unknown to the author, and all the incidents
are pure invention.

First published in Great Britain 2012
by Mills & Boon, an imprint of Harlequin (UK) Limited.
Large Print edition 2012
Harlequin (UK) Limited, Eton House,
18-24 Paradise Road, Richmond, Surrey TW9 1SR

© Leonie Knight 2012

ISBN: 978 0 263 22487 0

Printed and bound in Great Britain
by CPI Antony Rowe, Chippenham, Wiltshire

THE DOCTOR, HIS DAUGHTER AND ME

Many thanks to Heather and Ian,
retired dairy farmers and a wonderfully
generous couple, who helped me
with the details of life on a farm.

Also for Shellee and Margaret.
You are truly inspirational.

PROLOGUE

DR TARA DENNISON closed her eyes, took several deep breaths and tried to relax as the physio's thumbs dug deep into both sides of her neck. She was close to tears but it had nothing to do with the massage. She'd decided she couldn't put it off any longer. She would tell Ryan tonight. And then they would both be free…free of the guilt, anguish and pain that held them together in a fragile relationship that had mercilessly sapped the strength from both of them over the past three months.

'Ouch,' she said as the pressure on her spine amplified and teetered on the edge of pain.

'You're tenser today than you usually are. Is there anything wrong? Soreness anywhere?'

Tara opened her eyes. She definitely wasn't about to reveal that *everything* was wrong. That she loved her husband so much there was no way she could deny him the future he deserved—the loving *perfect* wife, sexual fulfilment, the children he'd always wanted…

'No, I'm fine. I think I may have overdone it in the gym yesterday. Perhaps we could call it quits now?'

'Good idea. I'll catch up with you in the pool tomorrow afternoon.'

'Yes, the pool…'

But before she had time to finish her sentence the physio had left, and a few minutes later she heard familiar footsteps heading towards her room. Her heart did a somersault and landed squarely in the pit of her stomach.

Now.

She'd made up her mind. She would definitely tell him *now*.

Ryan felt good. The time was right. He clutched an enormous bouquet of delicately scented yellow roses in one hand and the list he'd laboured over for the past week in the other. With the information he had, and Tara's all-time favourite flowers, how could she possibly refuse?

But when he reached her room, drew back the curtain and saw the expression on her face, he began to have doubts.

'Hi, beautiful.' He placed the flowers on the bedside table, leaned forward and kissed his wife on the mouth, holding the simple but intimate connection for as long as he could. Her mouth was immobile, her lips cool, and when he finally drew away her sombre expression flattened his mood like a burst balloon.

'What's the matter?'

She was looking at the roses as if he'd given her a bunch of stinging nettles.

'I have something I want to tell you.'

'That's great.' His gentle smile did nothing to thaw the icy expression on Tara's face. 'I have something to tell you too.'

Some of his previous joy at finally tying up all the loose ends of his plan that would give them the chance of a rosy future returned. His love for Tara had never waned. They had survived a horrific accident and were both miraculously alive; he'd been there every step of the way through the lengthy and arduous rehabilitation programme; he'd supported her through bouts of debilitating depression and he'd found a way for them to live out the happily-ever-after of their dreams. If she'd just let him explain…

'I'll go first.' The list he had made seemed redundant now, but he knew once she'd realised they weren't stuck in an inescapable rut…

'No, Ryan. Let me.'

Her eyes, which were usually wide open windows to her feelings, were shuttered.

'Okay,' he said slowly as he reached for her hand, but she snatched it away.

'I want a divorce.'

Ryan shook his head in disbelief. Just when there was a possibility they could get their lives back on track? Had he heard wrong?

'No!' The word came out more forcefully than he'd planned. 'Sorry,' he added, and this time Tara let him hold her hand. She was shaking.

'Why?'

She took a deep breath and looked him straight in the eye.

'Because I'm disabled, Ryan. I'm a different person to the perfect woman you married. I think and feel differently and I could never be a mother to your children—'

'But…' He squeezed Tara's hand tight. 'But none of that matters…if we love each other.'

Tara looked away and shifted restlessly in her hospital bed.

'Tara? Love…it's what has sustained us through the bad times as well as the good.'

Tara's gaze swung back to Ryan. She sighed.

'That's the problem, Ryan. I don't love you any more. And I can't live in a loveless marriage.' She cleared her throat. 'I want a divorce and I'm not going to change my mind.'

CHAPTER ONE

Eight years later.

RYAN DENNISON wasn't trying to avoid the inevitable confrontation, just delaying it. He circled the car park looking for an inconspicuous space from where he'd still have full view of the entrance to the clinic.

How long had it been since he'd seen Tara? He did a quick mental calculation. It was nearly eight years. Back then, he'd told her he was prepared to be there for her all the way, no matter the sacrifices. He'd had a workable plan for their future. But she'd insisted she wanted a divorce. He thought he'd found a way to overcome all their problems but he'd had no answer to her simple statement: *I don't love you any more.* And she'd been right; they couldn't stay together in a marriage without mutual love.

After several weeks of agonising self-doubt, guilt and pleading with Tara, she'd held her ground and become more distant as time went on. He knew her grief had been as gut-wrenching as his, but she hadn't seemed to understand the anguish he'd suffered at being pushed away, at having to endure years of remorse.

Yes, he'd agreed to end their marriage, but his heart still bore the scars of being rejected by the woman he'd loved with his whole being. His attempts to contact her by e-mails and phone calls in the first few years had been ignored, as if she'd been frightened of having any communication with him. His phone calls to her home phone had always been coldly blocked by her parents, who'd told him their daughter didn't want to talk to him, and she must have recognised his mobile number as his texts and calls went unanswered. In the end he'd stopped trying.

No one was to blame.

Well, that was what he'd kept telling himself— until the words almost lost their meaning.

But Tara's parents didn't believe it and he suspected Tara nursed doubts as well.

He parked the car and then glanced at his watch— four twenty-five. He'd done his homework. She finished at four-thirty but he'd come prepared for a wait. She would be busy, popular and almost certainly run overtime. Scanning the cars in the disabled section, he came to the conclusion hers would be the people-mover—the only vehicle big enough to take an electric wheelchair and be fitted with the gadgetry for a paraplegic driver.

Paraplegic… Oh, God, if only things had been different. Despite his outward calm he still had nightmares, replaying the horrors of that terrible evening. In the past week he'd woken nearly every night in a lather of torment, grief and with a vivid image of twisted metal. It was a painful reminder of how he was feeling about seeing his ex-wife again.

He took a sip of bottled water to cool the burning dryness in his throat.

He couldn't change the past. Now he was going to be working in the same building with her he hoped she'd at least talk to him. But unless she'd had a turnaround in her personality she'd be stubborn and cling fiercely to her independence. The fact she'd finished her training and found a job was testament to her determination. She didn't need—or want—him any more. She'd made that clear when they parted.

The guilt stabbed painfully again.

He closed his eyes for a moment and when he opened them he saw her, just as beautiful as she'd been the day he'd met her. The years had been kind to her. Her strawberry-blonde hair, streaked with gold, was cut shorter, so it fell in tapered wisps to her shoulders. He could see her arms were muscular and her shoulders a little broader than he remembered, but it didn't detract from her femininity. Grimacing with concentration, she skilfully manoeuvred to the driver's side of the vehicle, opened the door and positioned the wheelchair so she could haul herself into the driver's seat. Then she smiled and said something to the young woman accompanying her, who opened the rear door and put the chair on a hoist which lifted it into the luggage space. The woman waved as she returned to the building and Tara reversed and drove slowly away.

What now?

He'd seen her. That had been pleasure, not pain. But he still had to speak to her. Tell her he was soon starting sessional work in the specialist rooms attached to her practice. What a strange turn of fate that the position of visiting orthopaedic surgeon had come up in Keysdale, of all places. As the most junior partner in his practice, without any country attachments, he'd been offered the job and been expected to take it. Initially he'd had doubts, as it would mean bringing up traumas of the past he'd thought he'd laid to rest, but after thinking long and hard he'd realised it might be a way of achieving closure to confirm Tara had no feelings for him.

And now he was back, and he didn't want to present her with any nasty surprises like approaching her in the car park. It would have to be at her home—her parents' home. He cringed at the thought of a reunion with the two people he'd believed had liked him and approved of his marriage to their only daughter. But after the accident they'd not bothered to hide their abhorrence of him. *They'd* blamed him and then callously ignored him. Or at least her father had.

If there was any other way…

He decided to have a coffee in one of the cafés in the main street, go through in his mind what he would say, and then drive the ten kilometres out of town to the Fielding farm. He couldn't put it off any longer.

'Is Dad still working?' Tara asked as her mother helped her into her wheelchair.

'Yep, but he should be here any minute. He's been fixing fences down near the creek and said he'd finish the job after milking.' Jane Fielding closed the back of the car and followed her daughter towards the homestead.

'How was your day, love?' her mother asked, as she did every afternoon when Tara came home from work. Tara loved her mother dearly, but sometimes felt smothered by her protectiveness and yearned for a home of her own.

But Tara was realistic; leaving the family home wasn't practical. She'd need a purpose-built unit and help from an able-bodied person for things that most people took for granted—like transferring to her chair, shopping in a supermarket, hanging out washing or gaining access to immediate help in an emergency. Of course there were ways around these difficulties, but even the most basic tasks took longer when you were confined to a wheelchair. She'd have to rethink her schedule to incorporate cooking, housework, washing and ironing—all the things her mother did without complaint. Her life wasn't perfect, but it was a better option than moving out on her own. She was used to the routine. And her parents had made sacrifices, including nearly losing the farm, to cater for her needs and extra expenses in the early years. She would probably never be able to repay them.

'Oh, you know—the same as usual; nothing out of the ordinary.' She parked next to the kitchen bench where her mother began preparing a late afternoon tea.

A moment later she heard the sound of her father's boots being flung into the corner of the veranda near the back door.

'I'm home,' he shouted unnecessarily. You'd have to be deaf as a farm gate not to notice his comings and goings. Her mother always said it was a *man thing*—slamming doors, throwing things like a ball to a hoop and stomping around like an army major.

'We're in the kitchen. Tara's just come home and I'm making tea.'

'Rightio.'

Tara laughed. The word was so old-fashioned but suited her father perfectly.

Jane put fresh-brewed tea and a plate of orange cake on the bench as Graham Fielding entered the room.

'Have you washed your hands?' Tara's mother was quick to ask—as she always did when Graham came in from working on the farm.

'Yes, I've washed my hands,' he said as he held them up for inspection, before kissing Tara on her forehead. 'How's my best girl?'

Tara frowned. She hated the way her father often treated her as if she was still his little girl.

'Fine, Dad.' She reached for her cup of tea as her mother passed the cake. 'How did you go with the fences?'

'All done, but I won't move the cows until after milking tomorrow morning.'

'Want a hand?'

Though she was quite able to handle a quad bike to get around the farm, and knew the routine of milking back to front, she guessed her father would say no. As he always did. She was sure she could manage most of the work from her wheelchair with a simple modification to raise her height. She'd developed strength in her arms and shoulders to rival any man's.

But her father had refused to let her near the dairy after the accident. He didn't seem to understand that her help would give him more time for the heavier work that neither Tara nor her mother could manage. For him, there was a non-negotiable line between men's and women's work that she'd almost given up trying to cross. His one concession was letting her mother help out now they could no longer afford to hire a dairyman.

'No, love. It won't take long, and you deserve your free time on the weekends.'

He had good intentions but was seriously lacking in subtlety. Another one of those *man things*, as her mother would say. He had no idea, though. She hardly needed to keep a social diary. Her life had settled into a comfortable equilibrium of work, home and the occasional outing to the shops or the pool at the physio's in Bayfield, fifty kilometres away. And at the end of her working days she hardly had any energy left to party.

Their conversation was interrupted by a car pulling up at the front of the house.

'Are you expecting visitors?' Graham glanced at his wife.

'Might be Audrey. She said she'd come round some time this week to return those preserving jars. But she usually drives around the back.'

A car door slammed and a few moments later there was a crisp knock on the front door. 'I'll go and see who it is,' she added.

Graham stood up, an imposing thick-set man of six foot three. 'No, I'll go. You get another cup of tea poured.'

Tara heard her father talking, but not what he was saying. She could tell he was angry by the sharp rise and fall of his voice. The visitor was male, that was all she could tell, and clearly unwelcome.

'Doesn't sound like Audrey,' her mother said with eyebrows raised.

They stilled at the sound of the front door slamming and her father clomping, barefoot, down the passage.

'Who's that?' Jane asked. She'd already poured a cup of tea for the visitor and looked disappointed.

'You don't want to know.' He scowled and shifted his gaze to Tara. 'It's Ryan.'

It took Tara a few moments to process the information.

'Ryan?' The word escaped as a husky whisper and didn't require an answer. She'd tried to put her feelings for her ex-husband on hold since their dramatic parting, but rarely a day went by without her thinking of him, dreaming of what life *could* have been if she'd not rejected him so coldly. She'd made the right decision, though. She'd heard Ryan had married again and started a family. She was happy for him.

But she'd never stopped loving him.

So she'd have to make sure she remained cool and detached and not let her true feelings show.

But why was he here? And why now? She felt her heart pumping as a film of sweat broke out on her forehead. She felt winded.

After all these years!

She took a deep breath and attempted a steady voice. Both her parents were looking at her, waiting for her reaction. She tried to restore her usual calm.

'Ryan Dennison?'

The angry fire in her father's eyes answered her question.

'He's waiting outside, insisting he talks to you, says he won't go until he's seen you.' He paused as if gauging her reaction. 'I'll send him away—even if it means running him off the property with the shotgun—'

'No, Dad, I'll see him.' Though the last person she wanted to see was her ex, she knew her father wasn't joking about the gun. 'I'll go outside. There's no need for him to come in.'

He seemed to accept her suggestion as a sign of her disapproval of her ex-husband and conceded.

'All right, but you be careful.'

Tara wasn't sure what her father meant.

At the time of their separation her thoughts had been clouded by the devastation of losing so much—the use of her legs, her career, the baby they'd so desperately wanted to make their family complete.

Ryan had had his whole life to live. She hadn't

wanted to take that away from him. He'd just started his specialist training in orthopaedics—his dream career. If he'd become her full-time carer, as he'd said he would, the future they'd planned before the accident would have been shattered. She'd felt she had little choice, especially in the early days when the pain had been so acute, and in retrospect she'd probably been depressed, not capable of making rational decisions. Back then there'd been no way she could have deprived Ryan of his dreams of a career, a happy marriage to a healthy wife and the children he had wanted so much.

The best thing had been to divorce. It had been easier that way. She hadn't wanted to find out if Ryan was capable of coping with living with a woman who was disabled. He'd always described her as *perfect in every way.*

But she wasn't *perfect* any more, not since the crash, and her scars were more than just physical. Yes, the sadness and pain, both physical and emotional, had lessened as the years passed, but memories still lingered of the man she'd loved with every part of her heart and soul.

Why was he here? The thought tumbled into her mind again.

She felt light-headed as she opened the door and

the familiar clawing of panic descended like thick smog. Her heart began to pound and she gagged on the taste of bile at the back of her throat. A shard of irrepressible fear mixed with long-suppressed hurt stabbed at her heart and threatened to take control of her mind.

She stopped in the doorway and began taking slow, deep breaths.

'What's the matter, Tara? Are you all right? You look pale.'

For a long moment she'd been so preoccupied with losing control in front of Ryan she'd forgotten where she was. By now it was too late. A man she hardly recognised crouched in front of her. This was a successful man in his mid-thirties, with thick brown hair clipped short, clean-shaven and dressed in a conservative charcoal-grey suit, white shirt and silver tie. He looked nothing like the relaxed young man she remembered.

She was beginning to feel normal again, but couldn't bring herself to smile. Her emotions were too raw. She felt the slowing of her heartbeat and the fuzziness clearing from her head.

He still had the same deep blue eyes, though, and right now they were full of concern.

'I'm fine,' Tara replied. She hated the fact she'd

let down her guard and revealed how vulnerable she could be before they'd even said hello. 'I just get a bit light-headed sometimes. It never lasts for more than a few minutes.' The tension in Ryan's face relaxed. 'Dad said you wanted to talk to me.'

Ryan stood up with an expression that was almost but not quite a smile.

Damn his charisma and amazing good looks. She was determined not to expose her emotions, though. He mustn't know she still had feelings for him, but already she knew the spark was still there.

At least he wasn't focused on her humiliating physical response to him. But that was the thing with panic attacks. She'd thought she had them beat but they could be triggered by the most unexpected and sometimes insignificant things.

'There's something I thought you needed to know.'

Her confidence was coming back.

'I'd better sit down.' Tara had become used to making jokes about her condition, to break the ice for people who weren't comfortable with her disability, but this time it didn't work. The frown on Ryan's face was set in stone.

'*You'd* better sit down, then.' She pointed towards an old swing seat suspended from the rafters. She now felt calm and in charge of the emotions which had threatened to be her undoing a few moments ago.

'Do you need any help?'

'No.'

She set the chair in motion and forced him to move out of the way. Finally he sat down on the swing opposite her chair.

'So, what is it you want to talk to me about that's so important you were prepared to brave Dad and his threat to run you off the property?'

Ryan smiled.

But it didn't last long.

'He said that?'

'Mmm, he did.' She paused a moment, wondering how much of the past she could raise without ramping up the tension that already buzzed in the air between them. On reflection, she realised she had nothing to lose. It wasn't as if she was trying to impress Ryan, and he was well aware of her parents' dislike for him.

Ryan gazed into her eyes and she jolted at the unexpected connection. The feeling was from the past—something that had been exclusive to them alone—an understanding that she and Ryan had used to consider a sign of their closeness.

But it served no purpose now. She wasn't going to reveal how she really felt.

He finally spoke.

'I'm going to be working down here. I start in two weeks in the new specialist rooms attached to your clinic.'

He stared, as if trying to gauge her reaction. And she produced the goods in the form of a violent blush. Her heart began to race again, but she was determined to keep her cool despite the overwhelming shock of his revelation.

'I thought it was better for you to know in advance, rather than just bumping into me at work one day.'

She swallowed and concentrated on the calm evenness of her breathing.

'You could've easily phoned.' She wondered at his motives. She'd not heard from this man for nearly six years—since he'd finally got the message she didn't want to be reminded of the past by his e-mails and calls. All she knew of him was through the medical grapevine—he was a successful orthopaedic surgeon, three years after they broken up he had remarried, and the last she'd heard he was overseas.

'I wanted to see you…'

Tara found that hard to believe.

'Why?' That gnawing pain in her heart that visited her every day was demanding an answer. Anger surfaced unexpectedly. 'Were you frightened of what you might see?'

Ryan looked genuinely hurt—a totally unanticipated reaction. She hadn't meant to be cruel, but her emotions were ruling what came out of her mouth.

'Sorry,' she muttered.

'No… You're absolutely right. I should have phoned. I didn't realise seeing you without warning would upset you.' His pupils dilated, which made their rim of blue the colour of bright sky reflected in black ice. 'I'm the one who should be apologising.'

She still wasn't quite sure why he'd gone to the trouble of driving all the way to Keysdale and then out to the farm. It wasn't the sort of visit a person would plan on the offchance. She suddenly felt resentful that he'd upset the ordered balance of her life.

He looked down at his hands clasped in his lap and said quietly, 'How are your parents?'

It was a question she wasn't expecting. She thought a moment before replying.

'You're not part of our lives any more. I'd describe Mum's attitude to you as ambivalent, and Dad… well…you saw what he was like when he answered

the door. But I don't think they actually hate you…
It's what happened—the accident—they both still
blame you for that.'

Ryan reached for Tara's hand but she snatched
it away. Seeing him was traumatic enough. She
didn't want any physical contact because…because
she wasn't sure how she'd react. The old desire she
thought she'd buried long ago was still there. It
frightened her.

'And you?'

Tara closed her eyes and took a deep breath. She
was hurting. Why was Ryan trawling through what
had happened so long ago? No one was to blame for
the accident. He was a good driver and had done
what most people would have—tried to avoid their
collision with a kangaroo. With devastating consequences. Her situation was a cross she had *chosen*
to bear without him, and up until ten minutes ago
she'd been managing perfectly okay.

She opened her eyes but didn't look at Ryan.

'You know I've never held you responsible.' She
sighed. 'It happened, it was regrettable, but I'm over
it and I think you should be too.'

Ryan brushed a piece of fluff from his sleeve.

'Of course you're right,' he said. 'But it isn't
enough to stop me feeling it was my fault. Can

you understand how difficult it is for me to see you like…?' The words seemed to stick in his throat and he swallowed.

Tara looked into the distance, trying to take on board what Ryan was saying. He was hurting too.

Neither of them could ever forget the crash and its aftermath, and sometimes Tara thought Ryan had been more damaged than she. His dreams had been blown apart—his career, the life they'd planned together, the children they'd so desperately wanted. They'd talked about her completing her GP training part-time. She'd been off the pill for a couple of months and the heartbreaking irony was that her period had been a week overdue. She'd planned on doing a home pregnancy test the following week, but the day after the accident she'd bled…and bled…and bled…

Another tragic loss.

It had been as if her lifeblood had drained from her, but she'd always put on a brave face.

Of course they both knew she was still physically capable of conceiving and bearing children. She'd assumed she was no longer sexually attractive to him, though, and even if she did have a child she would need help to look after it. With the long hours Ryan worked she would be effectively a single parent. Combined with her disability, the whole scenario was unworkable.

To her alarm, she was close to tears. She needed to change the direction of the conversation.

'So you'll be doing sessional work, I guess?'

He also seemed grateful for the change of subject.

'I'll be operating on Thursdays and consulting Fridays, with the option to do an extra theatre session on alternative Saturday mornings. I'll stay overnight.'

'Where are you planning to stay?' she asked, purely out of curiosity.

'I thought one of the motels. But if you can suggest anything better?'

She thought for a moment.

'The Riverside is the best of the three motels in town. It's off the highway and not far from the clinic.' That was all the advice she was prepared to give.

'Right. I'm staying over tonight, so I can check out the consulting rooms and meet with the manager to go through all the paperwork tomorrow morning. I can book in to the motel you suggested. I plan to head back about lunchtime.'

To his wife.

Tara wondered what she would think of her hus-

band working away. But she certainly wasn't going
to delve into his personal life.

'Can I pick you up and take you out to lunch before I leave?'

No way! What on earth was he thinking?

Tara tried not to let her disbelief show on her face
and mustered a smile.

'No, thanks, I'm busy all day tomorrow,' she lied.
'And I'm sure you'll be keen to get home to your
wife and family.'

'Pardon?'

Hadn't he heard her or didn't he understand?

'You'll surely want to get home,' she repeated.

'To my wife and kids?'

Tara nodded.

'That's what I thought you said.' His brow crinkled in a frown. 'Of course—I shouldn't have assumed you'd know.'

'Know what?'

'Shannay and I divorced over a year ago and she
has custody of our daughter.'

He was waiting for a reaction but what did he expect? Should she express regret at the breakdown
of his second marriage? This was too much for her
to deal with. She'd had the idea, set in her mind,
that Ryan would find the perfect woman, that he

would have the perfect family. But divorce! It had never been in the equation.

'Sorry,' she finally said. 'I heard you'd married again, but—'

'To separate was the best option for both of us. We weren't compatible and it wasn't working out,' he muttered.

He stood to leave. He was obviously uncomfortable talking about it.

'I'll get going, then,' he added.

'Yes. I work Tuesday, Wednesday and Friday. so I'll probably bump into you when you start your Friday sessions.'

Before she had a chance to recoil he leaned down and placed a brief kiss on her cheek, and his questioning eyes lingered on hers for a moment before he strode down the steps and headed for his car.

He'd certainly changed, but in a lot of ways was still the same Ryan Dennison she'd fallen in love with. That was all in the past, though, dead and buried.

But he was single.

Of course that didn't alter anything, did it?

Seeing Tara again was like a rebirth.

Ryan had to deal with all the raw emotion, the

painful memories, the turmoil of indecision he'd held inside for so long. To overcome the reality of the wretched, haunting past that intruded into his dreams, that followed him during every waking hour of every day, was a challenge he wasn't sure he was ready for.

Did he blame himself?

How could he not?

He'd had control, he'd been at the wheel and his reflex reaction had resulted in the horrendous collision that had left Tara without the use of her legs.

The moment he'd realised Tara's future had been snatched away from her he'd desperately wanted to turn back the clock. If he'd seen the kangaroo twenty seconds earlier, if he'd reacted faster, if the massive tree had been a few metres further along the road, if they'd left the party ten minutes earlier, if he hadn't insisted they stop to buy a bottle of wine on the way home, if he could change places with her, if… There were so many ifs he thought he'd dealt with, but deep down he still nursed a guilt that was so sharp, it cut directly into his heart.

Visiting Tara had made him wish he'd tried harder to convince her she'd been more important to him than a career or money or a tribe of kids. He'd felt sure they could pick up the pieces, but had been rejected when Tara had told him her love had dried up. He'd been devastated, but in the end had genuinely believed he'd done what was best for them, what Tara wanted. She'd not wanted to even give him a chance to provide the love and caring he'd thought only he could give. Tara had been determined and immovable in her resolve that getting a divorce was the only way she could put the past behind her.

And, in a way, she'd been right.

She now had a fulfilled life with a satisfying job and she was more beautiful than ever. It wouldn't surprise him if she had dozens of admirers and could have the pick of the bunch. In fact Ryan was surprised she hadn't remarried.

But that was her business.

He had no right to interfere with what she'd worked so hard to achieve.

It wouldn't be easy, but he'd just have to ignore the churning deep in his belly and the ache in his heart and get on with his own life. Thinking that there was even the remotest chance they could get back together was an aberration. Tara's attitude to him had verified that.

Ryan slowed down as he reached the outskirts of the town. He suddenly felt exhausted. It had been a long day and he'd had an early start, which made the prospect of a hot cup of coffee and a soft bed very attractive.

The Riverside Motel, Tara had said.

He travelled slowly through Keysdale's sleepy town centre until he saw a sign pointing east towards the river. After about half a kilometre the motel came into view, and he shifted his focus from ruminations about Tara to the practicalities of organising his accommodation for the night.

Two rows of tidy units nestled on the banks of the Keysdale River. Most had views of the lush green paddocks beyond and it was quiet, away from traffic noise and had an air of relaxed tranquillity about it.

He pulled up in front of the office, got out of his black sports car and stretched. He'd done too much driving that afternoon, and his right hip ached from the bursitis he got when he sat for too long. A bell above the office door tinkled as he opened it but there was no one inside. He gazed around, noting the tourist brochures advertising the history museum, a dairy called The Milk Factory, white-water rafting and half a dozen local restaurants.

He took a double-take and grabbed a leaflet, but before he had a chance to look at it more closely a plump, middle-aged woman emerged from a back room.

She smiled and greeted him.

'Hello, sir. Do you want a room?'

'Yes, just for tonight.' He explained his requirements for regular accommodation and they came to an arrangement.

'Here's your key. Your room's nice and quiet with a wonderful view.' She paused to take a breath. 'Dinner is served from six-thirty to eight-thirty and there's a menu in your room for breakfast orders.'

'Thank you.'

The woman glanced at the leaflet he was still clutching in his hand.

'Well worth a visit if you've time.'

'Maybe next time,' he said as he turned to leave.

'Enjoy your stay, Mr Dennison.'

'I'm sure I will,' he said cheerily, trying to convince himself, but he knew he'd spend most of his spare time soul-searching.

Before he climbed into his car he had a closer look at the brochure.

THE MILK FACTORY.

EXPERIENCE A WORKING DAIRY FARM FIRST HAND

Ten kilometres south of Keysdale, on Hill Park Road.

He scrutinised the photo then unfolded the leaflet.

Open for tours. Devonshire teas.
10 a.m. to 5 p.m. weekends and public holidays
Dairy tours including real-life milking 3 p.m.
Proprietors: Graham and Jane Fielding

He hadn't even noticed.

There would have been signs. How could he have missed them? He must have been so focused on seeing Tara he'd been oblivious to anything else.

But it made him think.

Were the Fieldings struggling to make ends meet?

Did Tara *have to* go out to work?

Did the accident have anything to do with their situation?

He felt discomfort in the pit of his stomach.

So much had changed in the years since he'd lost contact with Tara and her family. His ex-wife certainly had.

He drove to his unit, grabbed his briefcase and overnight bag and let himself in. He rummaged in a tiny cupboard above the sink, found a sachet of instant coffee and filled the kettle. When the brew was made, he opened the sliding door which led to the veranda. The setting sun cast long shadows across the river and a cow's gentle mooing echoed in the quiet. He seemed to have the place to himself.

With time to think.

About Tara.

It was impossible to erase her, and all the reasons he'd fallen in love with her more than a decade ago, from his mind.

She was even more beautiful than he remembered, and her fighting spirit had not been dulled by circumstance or time.

It suddenly occurred to him that he'd found out what he needed to know—he still loved her.

But he didn't have the faintest idea what to do about it.

After Ryan left, Tara needed some alone time to gather her thoughts, so she stayed on the veranda and watched a golden sun sink slowly towards the horizon.

Why?

Why now?

She'd mourned her decision to send Ryan away every day. The flame of her love for him still burned brightly, and seeing him again… It was like a dam bursting—as if time had stood still for those eight years and suddenly she was looking into the eyes of the man who, for her, would always be her soul mate.

How should she react?

He was divorced, but there was no way they could start again. She had a satisfying life she'd worked hard to achieve and Ryan had his life in the city. It shouldn't be difficult to act cool and detached and very professional. After all she would rarely see him.

Yes…cool, detached and professional. She could do that.

Couldn't she?

CHAPTER TWO

'THE new orthopaedic surgeon starts today,' said Kaylee, the young receptionist, as she operated the pneumatic lift that moved Tara's wheelchair from her vehicle and placed it on the ground. Tara preferred to use her electric chair at work, as it provided greater manoeuvrability, but getting it on and off her vehicle was one of the few things she couldn't manage herself and had reluctantly learned to live with.

'I know.' Tara had been counting the days and psyching herself up for her first meeting with Ryan in the workplace. None of the staff were aware of her history with him. Of course some of the close-knit community knew she'd been married, but Ryan was a city man, born and bred. He'd hated the idea of any kind of fuss and had always been a reluctant participant in their rare visits to the farm. And, the way she was feeling right now, it was a good thing. She didn't want the burden of gossip to stress her any more than she was already. She certainly wasn't prepared for a public airing of her past, which she'd spent the best part of the last eight years trying to forget.

Not yet. Not today.

She'd also had time to think about his visit to the farm two weeks ago and had pondered on his motives. In fact she'd questioned long and hard about why he would choose a job in Keysdale when not only did he hate rural life but he probably had the pick of any position he wanted?

The questions burned and she needed some answers…from Ryan.

Her thoughts were interrupted by the young receptionist.

'And Jenny said he's gorgeous.'

Kaylee positioned the wheelchair next to the driver's seat and stood back as Tara used the strength in her arms to shift into it. The girl seemed oblivious to the flush of embarrassment that warmed Tara's cheeks and prattled on.

'Jen met him when he came down a couple of weekends ago. She said he's really nice, as well as good-looking.'

'What about the paediatrician? Isn't she starting today as well?'

Tara was desperate to change the subject. She

didn't need to know that her ex-husband had already charmed at least one of the female staff, and probably the whole Saturday morning team.

'Yeah, this afternoon. Val's putting on a special lunch to welcome them both, and she's asked their receptionist not to overbook on the first day so they'll have time to meet us all.'

'Oh.'

Tara had prepared herself for the possibility that she'd bump into Ryan at some stage during the day. The brand-new specialist offices, although housed in an extension to the GP clinic building, were separate and self-contained. They had their own reception area, procedure room and consulting suites, but the lunch room was shared. She'd planned to eat a sandwich in her room and catch up with her paperwork, but that wasn't an option now. She'd be expected to make an appearance, at least.

Kaylee walked beside her as she steered through the self-opening doors and made her way to the busy waiting area, past Reception then to the doctors' rooms beyond.

'See you later,' the teenager said as their paths diverged.

Tara nodded and forced a smile, eager to reach the privacy of her consulting room so she could take a minute or two to compose herself. She'd never had a panic attack at work and she wasn't about to change that today.

Ryan scanned the room full of chattering staff but couldn't see Tara. He lingered a moment in the doorway, taking in the table laden with a bounty of home-cooked food, but was soon approached by the principal doctor at Keysdale Medical Clinic, Rob Whelan. The man greeted Ryan with a welcoming grin.

'I'll introduce you to the mob, and then you can eat…' his grin broadened '…and mingle.'

Rob reeled off a long list of names Ryan would never remember to associate with the endless stream of nodding, smiling faces. Then, his gaze automatically following his colleague's, he turned, and it was as if the waters parted. People moved out of the way as Tara wheeled herself into the room with a barely suppressed scowl on her face and rosy colour in her cheeks.

'And last but not least…' Rob said, resting his hand lightly on Tara's shoulder. 'Dr Tara Fielding.' He glanced at Ryan. 'This is Ryan Dennison, our new visiting orthopaedic surgeon.'

Thank God Tara had reverted to her maiden

name, averting a possible problem he hadn't thought of until now.

At that moment Rob's attention was taken by the timely arrival of Karin Hooper, the new paediatrician. Rob began the introduction ritual all over again, and Ryan was grateful the spotlight had moved away from him and Tara, who was still right next to him, waiting for her turn in the short queue for the food. She reluctantly shook his offered hand as he leaned over to talk to her.

'I'm glad to finally meet you, Dr Fielding. I've heard so much about you.' It was an attempt at humour to lighten Tara's mood but he wasn't sure if it had worked.

She answered him with a cool smile as she released his hand from a momentary grip of steel.

'Ouch,' he couldn't help exclaiming.

'Sorry.' She was grinning now but still looked tense…guarded. 'Sometimes I forget my own strength.' She picked up two plates and handed one to Ryan, who promptly discarded the fleeting thought of offering to serve her food. He had much to learn.

'How has your day been so far? Not too snowed under with Keysdale's unique brand of orthopaedic problems?' It was inconsequential small talk.

He laughed politely. 'You mean crush fractures from being stepped on by livestock and strain injuries from overdosing on fencing?'

'You've got the idea.'

While he was talking Ryan watched in wonder as Tara effortlessly multi-tasked, deftly moving her chair into impossibly small spaces while at the same time loading her plate with enough to feed a professional athlete.

She paused a moment and looked at his empty plate.

'Aren't you hungry?' she asked.

'Oh…er…yes.' He stuttered his reply, not prepared to admit he'd been too busy watching her. After shouldering his way through the tightly packed occupants of the small lunch room, he began to select food from the abundance before him. By the time he'd filled his plate Tara had moved to the other side of the room and was deep in conversation with a woman he remembered, from her name tag, was a physiotherapist.

Balancing his plate in one hand, he headed in Tara's direction but was stopped midway by a tap on his shoulder. He turned.

'Sorry to desert you,' Rob Whelan said amiably. 'I wanted to have a word with you about the possibility of you doing some extra consulting—maybe on the Saturday mornings you're not operating?'

If Ryan's appointment book was anything to go by, the services of an orthopaedic surgeon in the town were desperately needed, but he was over-committed as it was.

'I'm sorry, I'm on call at St Joseph's one week-end in four, and…' He hesitated, deciding whether Rob, a relative stranger, needed to know about the custody arrangements he had for access to his daughter. As it was, he only saw her one weekend a month, and that time was precious.

If things had been different… He sighed.

'And?' Rob raised his eyebrows, as if he sensed Ryan's discomfort but his curiosity overrode tact. Maybe it was the country way—that everyone had a God-given right to know everyone else's business. But it wasn't Ryan's way.

'I have regular family commitments on most of my free weekends.' His use of the word *free* was somewhat tongue-in-cheek, but the vague comment was all he was prepared to give at the moment. 'And I think you'll find things will settle down in a month or two, once I work through the backlog of referrals and start seeing follow-ups.'

Rob rubbed his chin and pressed his mouth into a thin line.

'I thought as much.' The older doctor's grin reappeared. 'But, you know, if your situation changes the offer stands.'

'I'll bear that in mind.'

At that moment Ryan noticed Tara heading off, and he wanted to talk to her. He felt oddly jilted. But he didn't have any claim on what she did.

'If you'll excuse me, I just want to...' His voice trailed off as one of the other GPs in the practice cornered Rob Whelan and let Ryan off the hook. Ryan dumped his barely touched food onto the table to follow Tara, but she'd vanished in the space of a few seconds. He went in pursuit and found her room off the corridor leading to Reception.

He knocked quietly but there was no response.

Maybe she hadn't gone back to her room.

He knocked again, a little louder.

'Tara?' He opened the door but her spacious office was empty. He glanced around and noted the modifications that had been made because of Tara's disability. Shelves and cupboards were no higher than shoulder-height. There were two patients' chairs but a notable absence of a seat for the doctor. The examination couch was also low, and the pedal that raised or lowered the bed had been modified to accommodate hand controls similar to those used for hospital beds. In fact just about everything in the room was reachable from a wheelchair.

He heard movement from behind a door on the far side of the room, and then the sound of a toilet flushing and water running. The door opened, apparently remote-controlled, and Tara wheeled herself into the room, concentrating on the small joystick that controlled the direction of her chair. She obviously hadn't seen him as he stood quietly by the door.

He cleared his throat and the muscles of Tara's shoulders visibly jerked. She scowled as blood rose to her neck and coloured her face.

'What the—?'

'Sorry, I knocked. Twice.' He cleared his throat again.

'Well, did you want to see me for something?' Tara said after they'd eyeballed each other for what felt like an age but was probably less than twenty seconds.

'I...'

What was supposed to be a relaxed greeting and a little ice-breaking chat on his first day working in the Keysdale clinic wasn't working out the way he'd planned.

'I just wanted to touch base…er…in a professional capacity, of course.' He smiled uneasily. It sounded ridiculous now. 'But you disappeared before I had time to say much more than hello just now.'

Tara tilted her head slightly and the steely look in her eyes blocked any access to what she was thinking. Then the expression on her face softened, as if she'd had a change of mind. It was too much to expect she'd had a change of heart.

'You took me by surprise,' she said bluntly. 'I have a fairly rigid routine at work. It means I can use my time here the most efficiently.' She hesitated.

'Oh, I'm sorry. I didn't mean to—'

'You weren't to know. After all, a good many years have passed since we last saw each other and a lot has happened since then. We've both been living our own lives and I'm not the same person I was back then.'

She was unable to hide her quick downward glance. He didn't blame her for being bitter. Thoughts that had been tumbling through his mind over the last two weeks returned.

*If he could change places with her, he would—a
hundred times over; if he could turn back the clock;
if only things had been different.*

He felt totally helpless.

'Yes.' It wasn't often Ryan was lost for words.
He was now.

Tara fiddled with some papers on her desk, arranging them in a neat pile. Then she repositioned
herself in her chair.

'Well, while you are here, have you a minute to
discuss a patient?'

'Yes, of course.'

The atmosphere had definitely lightened. The tension of discussing the past evaporated like summer
rain falling on hot asphalt.

'Her name's Pippa Morgan and I've asked her
to make an appointment to see you but it could be
a couple of weeks down the track. I've been told
how busy you are, and that you're booked up for
the next month.'

'Tell me about her.'

Tara swung around to face him.

'She's nineteen. Juvenile rheumatoid arthritis was
diagnosed when she was six years old. She's been
managed by a rheumatologist from the early stages.'
Tara paused to take a breath. 'Of course I've only

known her as a teenager, and she's been under the care of Liam Taylor for the past two years. She's had just about every treatment in the book to control her pain and inflammation—non-steroidal anti-inflammatories, Prednisone, Methotrexate, a trial of a DMARD as well as joint injections.'

Ryan had treated many patients with the inflamed and sometimes deformed joints of the chronic rheumatic condition rheumatoid arthritis, but rarely saw children or young adults with the disease. Treatment by surgery was usually kept in reserve for when all else failed. And the bulk of his experience had been with the middle-aged and elderly.

'Liam's one of the best adult rheumatologists around.'

'It was he who suggested she may need a hip replacement in the next year or two.'

'And you want my opinion?'

'That's right.'

Their conversation was interrupted by Ryan's mobile phone. He answered the call from his receptionist.

'Sorry, there's an emergency. A child with what sounds like displaced fractures of tib and fib.' He looked at his watch and noted his busy afternoon consulting was due to start as well. 'I'm going to have to go.'

'Of course.'

'We'll talk about Pippa later.' He paused in the doorway on his way out. 'I'll ring you.'

As Ryan strode down the corridor he tried to file thoughts of Tara Fielding deep in the back of his mind so he could focus totally on his work.

'I'm taking two patient files with me tonight. Also, would you mind checking if we have a referral letter for a nineteen-year-old named Pippa Morgan—and have you typed out the theatre list for tomorrow?' Ryan glanced at the wall clock behind his receptionist, eager to leave. He'd had an early start and a long day.

Liz extracted a file from the cabinet and leafed through a dozen sheets of paper before she found the letter Ryan had asked for.

'Here it is. I'd have remembered if I'd scanned it into the computer records because I'd have made a file for her.' She stood up. 'I'll just do you a photocopy.'

The efficient middle-aged woman smiled. She was a Keysdale local, and today was the first time he'd met her, but she'd certainly proved her worth.

She seemed to have the ability to think and act one step ahead of him.

'So you don't trust me to return it?'

'I'm sure you have the best of intentions but I know how busy doctors are.'

'And it might get overlooked?' He returned her smile.

'Something like that.' She handed him the copy of the letter as well as the theatre list, and jotted down the names of the patient files he'd laid on the counter. 'And there's one more thing.'

'What's that?'

'I won't be a moment,' she said as she turned and headed for the back room, returning with a loaded plastic carry-bag. 'You won't need to think about what to eat this evening. There was so much food left over from the welcome party, and the girls didn't want to waste it. Someone noticed you rushed off without touching your lunch so they thought you were a worthy recipient.'

Ryan took a quick peek in the bag and noted there was enough food to last for the next week.

'Thanks, that's a really kind thought, but I can't possibly eat all of this.'

'It'll only get thrown away, so you might as well take it.' He took the bag.

'Okay, thanks, Liz. I'll see you next week, then.'

When he arrived in the car park he offloaded the food and his gear in the back seat, climbed in and turned the key in the ignition. But instead of firing on the first turn the engine groaned and his state-of-the-art luxury car gave up.

'Damn, this is the last thing I need,' he muttered. He tried again with the same result, wondering if his usually reliable car had been interfered with. 'The last thing I need…' he muttered again, trying one more time to fire up the engine.

He phoned his roadside call-out service and was given the number of a local auto repair shop. When the mechanic arrived the news was not good.

During Tara's busy afternoon every patient seemed to take longer than their allotted time, and at the end of her list she was running nearly an hour late. It was well past five o'clock. If she was running too late her parents worried. She understood why. The accident had fuelled what had become their almost obsessive concern about the safety of their only child, their precious, perfect, beautiful daughter—but it didn't make her life any easier. No matter how many times she'd tried to persuade them she was capable of looking after herself they still waited up for her when she had the occasional date or night out with her friends. And she had to tell them where she was going, especially if she was driving on her own.

Right now she had to live with it. Tara owed her parents big-time and she didn't want to cause them any more stress than they already had.

She packed her things in readiness to leave and headed to Reception. When she was barely out of her room Ryan burst through the outside door as if he was being pursued by a pack of rabid dogs. He'd certainly found a novel way of attracting attention.

'Is there a taxi service in this town?' he said in a voice laced with frustration and impatience.

Tara wheeled slowly closer, but Ryan hadn't noticed her and went on without waiting for a reply.

'My car won't start. There's something wrong with the ignition system and it needs to be towed to the local garage to be repaired—'

'I've got some jump leads in my car if that's any help,' Jenny offered.

Ryan sighed. 'I wish... Apparently the computer and security system is so complicated you need an auto electrician to reset and reconnect it, even if it's simply a flat battery. Which won't happen until tomorrow.'

Some of the edginess had gone from Ryan's voice and he looked worn out. He'd obviously had a busy day and it appeared it wasn't going to get any better.

Tara was at the counter now.

'I'm just leaving and can drop you off. Taxis here are notoriously unreliable unless you make an advance booking. Where are you staying?'

Ryan looked stunned, as if Tara was the last person he'd expected to see, let alone offer a simple solution to his predicament.

'Ahh…'

Three sets of eyes were fixed on him, waiting for a reply, and Tara began to wonder if her offer was a mistake.

'You could help me with my chair.' Tara was the one to break the uncomfortable silence.

'I'm at the Riverside. I could probably walk, but I have a lot of gear to transport.' He hesitated. 'And it would just be for tonight. A hire car is being delivered to the motel in a couple of hours.' His expression softened. 'Thanks, Dr Fielding.'

When they reached her car Tara couldn't help noticing Ryan's gaze drift to her legs and then to the hand controls of the car. Suddenly she felt she had something to prove to Ryan—that she could manage perfectly without him. She didn't want pity, or sympathy, or even admiration. She just wanted her ex-husband to accept her for who she was.

'What do I need to do to get your chair into the car?' he said, after he'd moved a couple of plastic crates, his medical case and two supermarket carry-bags from the boot of his now useless car to the back seat of her vehicle.

Good. The practicality of the transfer from chair to car was the perfect diversion from thoughts of Ryan encroaching on her personal space. She wheeled close to the driver's door, opened it and lifted herself into the seat.

'When you open the back you'll see the platform. The controls are hooked onto the driver side just below the window.'

Ryan was already at the rear of the vehicle. He opened the door.

'Is this it?' He waved the handpiece.

'Yes. All you have to do now is press the down arrow button and the platform is programmed to slide out and down to the ground. Simply strap the chair in and press the up button.

'Ah, yes, I can see it.'

A few seconds later he was at her side. 'Is there anything else I can do?'

'Thanks, but I can manage now.'

Tara felt her jaw tighten, and her words did little to disguise her feelings, which were churning around like a newspaper caught in a whirlwind. She'd had no idea being in close proximity to Ryan—alone—would have such an unsettling effect on her. She'd programmed herself to keep him at a distance and now he was sitting a handspan away from her.

At that moment she wondered if she'd made a mistake. She wished she could drive straight home.

But she couldn't.

Though Ryan was grateful for Tara's offer to help him out, he got the impression she wished she was anywhere but sitting next to him in her car.

What could he do to help her relax? After all it wasn't his fault his car had broken down and she'd offered him the lift. She might be taking him back to his motel, but it wasn't as if he then expected her to sleep with him…

Where had that come from?

The thought did hold some attraction, though. He glanced in her direction and dismissed the idea from his mind. The scowl on Tara's face suggested she'd more likely suffer being thrown into a pit of deadly snakes than have the slightest physical contact with him.

But why?

He'd been pleasant and polite without being over-friendly. He'd made no demands on her, and he hoped he'd dealt with his ex-wife in a non-confrontational way.

But she'd changed. The openness they'd always shared in their relationship had been replaced by a cautious hesitancy; the love of life she'd had in bucketloads seemed to have dried up; taking risks and trying new things had been supplanted by the rigid routine enforced by her disability. And she certainly wasn't to blame. No one was to blame. Ryan repeated the words that had become a mantra in the months following the accident.

No one was to blame.

Did Tara believe that?

He truly wanted to find out and, if the barriers were still up, shielding the intimacy they'd had in the past, then maybe he should just try for friendship. Now he had seen her again he knew he at least needed to talk to her. And perhaps he had the ideal opportunity tonight. After all, the worst that could happen was that she'd simply refuse, and he could live with that.

They were pulling into the driveway of the motel so he didn't have much time.

'I really appreciate you helping me out, Tara. Can I repay you for the lift?'

'Pardon?' She glanced briefly in his direction before bringing the car to a halt in front of the office.

'I want to repay you.'

'What do you mean?' Her stare was ice-cool.

'Liz gave me some leftovers from lunch and I have way too much to eat myself. Would you like to share them with me?'

The stare turned into a frown and then she looked straight ahead, moving the gearstick from 'Park' to 'Reverse'.

'Which unit is yours?'

Any kind of thaw seemed a long way away, and Ryan accepted the fact he'd just been handed a refusal. Nothing lost, nothing gained.

But then her expression changed. Still cool but the ice was melting.

'Okay. I have that patient I mentioned earlier I wanted to discuss with you. Would you mind—?'

'Of course not.' Ryan had the feeling he had nudged a little closer to first base.

And what could be more innocent than two colleagues discussing a patient over a bite to eat? Tara shouldn't feel threatened by that. Ryan's face broke into a smile as he realised what he'd thought was going to be a gloomy end to his long day had the potential to shine.

CHAPTER THREE

PART of the reason for Tara's decision to share a meal with Ryan was because over the last two weeks, since he'd catapulted back into her life, she'd been thinking about him constantly. She also had some questions she needed answering, and it wasn't the sort of discussion that could take place in the lunch room at the clinic.

Her all-consuming concern was…why?

Why was he back when she'd worked so hard to make her life as good as it could be without him?

Why had he accepted a job in Keysdale when he could choose any job he wanted?

Why had he married, fathered a child and then divorced a few short years later?

And the last question she could only answer herself—why did she care so much when she'd thought she was well and truly over him?

She tried to rationalise by telling herself it was perfectly reasonable that she held a gnawing suspicion about his motives. But were those emotions that were surfacing from another time in her life an indication she still had feelings for her ex-husband?

It scared her.

She was also annoyed that her balanced, well-ordered world was beginning to tilt on its axis a little. Her life was complicated enough as it was and she didn't need any more problems.

To clear the air she definitely needed to at least talk to Ryan, so she could clarify her own feelings. All she knew now was that the man sitting next to her with a genuine smile on his face, had forced her to revisit a time when she'd been married to the only man she'd truly loved. While he'd been married to a stranger, settled more than two hundred kilometres away and living the life she'd always hoped he'd have, she'd overcome the pain and uncertainty of wondering if he sincerely believed, as he'd told her a hundred times after the accident, *she* was more important than anything else in his life.

Ryan cleared his throat as he opened the car door and she wondered if he'd been watching her.

'I'll get your chair and then I'll unload all my stuff.'

'Thanks,' she said quietly, forcing a smile.

Ryan was a quick learner. In just a few minutes he had the chair where she could easily transfer into it and was rummaging in the back of the car, unpacking his bags and boxes.

'Would you mind carrying the food?'

'Fine.' He definitely did learn fast, and was doing his best not to make a big thing of what Tara *couldn't do* and focusing on what she *could.*

After locking the vehicle, Tara propelled herself to the small entry of Ryan's unit and waited while he unlocked the door, went inside and turned on the lights. She cast a quick glance around the compact living-dining area and noted that her host was obviously not expecting guests. The small desk in one corner was littered with papers and a large overnight bag decorated the single settee. She could see jeans and a couple of tee shirts strewn on the bed, with a cup and a juice box sitting on the bedside table. At least the bathroom door was closed. She didn't want to conjure up any thoughts of Ryan that tipped outside the boundaries she'd decided to impose for any contact outside work.

'Sorry about the mess.'

Ryan's clichéd reply brought a small smile to Tara's face. He'd always been messy.

Ryan put the food in the kitchen, stowed the rest of his gear in the bedroom and closed the door. He was staring at her intently.

'What's so amusing?'

Damn. She'd let her guard down. She restored what she hoped was a neutral expression. The last thing she wanted to do was to tell Ryan her thoughts.

'Nothing at all. However, I should ring my parents and let them know I'll be home late.

'Yes, of course you must. I'll go and get changed while you do and then we'll eat.'

Tara watched him disappear into the bedroom and sighed, hoping she'd have the courage to start to put her life back on course. She rang her parents' number.

As Ryan pulled on a pair of jeans and a crumpled polo shirt a jumble of thoughts he'd previously managed to suppress scuttled through his mind.

Thoughts of the past.

He now realised that his years with Tara had been the best of his life, but she'd changed; her body had changed. Ryan knew it shouldn't make any difference but it did. Although *his* feelings for *her* were strong, Tara was guarded and cautious around him. He didn't seem to be able to get it right—the balance between friendly helpfulness and the undeniable protectiveness he felt for her. She seemed to want to be treated only as a colleague, but he couldn't ignore their past.

He was responsible for the way things were now. The thought kept flashing in his mind like a neon sign that wouldn't go away.

It added to his remorse.

In the end, he decided to let the evening chart its own course and he'd suffer any consequences. After all, it was unlikely they'd have the opportunity to spend much time together at work. Already he had a good idea he'd have little spare time to socialise during the couple of days he spent each week at Keysdale. In fact he'd been prepared for a knock-back when he'd asked Tara to share a meal with him.

Tara… She was rapidly turning into an enigma. He remembered how self-contained she'd been when he'd watched her get in her car and drive away without any idea he was in the car park on that Friday afternoon a couple of weeks ago. But he'd also seen traces of anxiety mixed with vulnerability during the brief contacts he'd had with her since. His natural instinct was to offer to help, but her independence stood firm as a barrier to his good intentions. He took a deep breath and opened the bedroom door. Tara had moved his bag and settled herself in one corner of the settee.

She glanced at him, blushed and then focused on the bags on the kitchen bench. She was more ill at ease than he was.

'The food smells delicious.'

Small talk was definitely a good idea.

'They seem like pretty high-quality leftovers. I hope you don't mind?' Ryan stood awkwardly, not sure what to do next. He began unpacking the food.

'Of course not.' She scrutinised every dish.

'Are you happy to eat now?'

'I don't mind. Whatever you want to do.'

Tension buzzed in the air. It was almost as if they were on a first date.

'I somehow managed to miss out on lunch and I'm starving.' He cleared his throat. 'My brain functions better on a full stomach.'

He began to lay out two place settings on the tiny kitchen gate-leg table, but then realised there would be more room on the coffee table.

'I'll spread the food out here. There's much more space and we can serve ourselves.'

'Yes, that's a sensible idea. I'm hungry.' She paused a moment, then smiled. 'I hope you don't mind women with hearty appetites.'

Ryan couldn't help doing a quick appraisal and it reinforced his first impressions. He was pleased with what he saw. Tara wore trousers and a tailored shirt with the top two buttons open, revealing a hint of cleavage which he hadn't noticed earlier in the day. Her upper body was lean and well toned. He imagined she exercised regularly to keep in shape.

She was an attractive woman...and very sexy.

His heart thudded uncomfortably at the realisation. Sex had been an important and joyous part of their relationship. Making love with Tara had always been a deeply sensual experience—he smiled—laced with a unique sense of fun that he'd never experienced with his second wife, Shannay. With the benefit of hindsight and the lingering pain of a second divorce, he realised his feelings for his second wife had been based on a blinding infatuation, probably arising from a need to escape his grief.

There was no hint Tara had any similar feeling towards him, though. She was looking at him impatiently, waiting for his reply.

'No, definitely not,' he said at last.

Once the food was set out they both loaded their plates and ate their fill.

When Tara put her empty plate on the table, Ryan

cleared the dishes and left them on the sink to deal with later.

He sat down next to Tara.

'So tell me about your patient.' It was neutral territory and unlikely to open any old wounds.

'Yes, of course.'

Focusing on something other than Ryan was exactly what Tara needed.

Reaching over to her wheelchair, where she'd left her bag, she extracted Pippa Morgan's file. She opened volume two to the section containing test results, investigation reports and specialist letters.

'Do you want a recap on her history?'

Ryan nodded. 'Good idea,' he said.

Tara repeated what she'd told Ryan earlier—that the teenager had suffered from the painful and debilitating condition of juvenile rheumatoid arthritis since early childhood, and that her joints had degenerated to the point where her specialist was considering the possibility of surgery to relieve the increasingly severe pain in her right hip.

'The rheumatologist has exhausted all the possibilities in his repertoire?'

'Yes, Pippa's had just about all medical treatments available. Even a course of injections of an experimental anti-metabolite. They worked for a while, but her liver started showing signs of stress.' Tara extracted a radiology report from the file. 'This is her latest X-ray report.' She paused as Ryan took the two sheets she handed him, containing a long and detailed assessment. 'The patient has the original films, but I've asked Pippa to bring her most recent X-rays when she comes to see you.'

Ryan was silent and his face immobile as he read the report. It was impossible to tell what he was thinking. Finally he looked up, his expression bleak.

'She's only nineteen. Poor kid,' he said softly as his brow furrowed into a frown.

'They're awful, aren't they? Her left hip is nearly as bad.'

Ryan nodded. 'About as bad as I've seen in someone so young.' He hesitated, closing his eyes and rubbing his forehead as if attempting to erase what he'd seen in the X-ray report. He took a deep breath as he opened his eyes. 'You know I mainly see adults?'

'Pippa is an adult. And a beautiful young person who has had to grow up fast,' Tara couldn't help adding. Against all that she'd been told in her training, Tara had developed a bond with Pippa that went beyond the usual relationship between doctor and patient. Their connection was all about shared disabilities which had robbed them of many things healthy, able-bodied people took for granted. Tara understood exactly what her young patient was going through. No matter how much they strived to live a normal life they would always be considered different, and often a burden to those who cared for them. And Pippa was a teenager, with all the baggage associated with her stage in life—the transition from childhood to adulthood; the need to be accepted by peers; rebellion against parental control; preoccupation with appearances and the related issues involving self-esteem, making choices about her future. The list was endless.

'You know what I mean,' Ryan answered.

'Sorry, of course I do. Anyone under fifty is young when it comes to considering a hip prosthesis.'

'Just based on the report, she must have a high level of pain and loss of joint function. And I agree the left hip doesn't look too great either.'

'The pain is the deciding factor for her. Some days it's an ordeal to get up in the morning, and her slow, stiff movements are more to do with the fact her joints are hurting so much than limitation due to the disease.'

'Quality of life?' Ryan asked with a sigh.

'She finished Year Twelve last year—amazing to be only a year behind her peers when she's had so much time off. She gained the marks to get into uni and has enrolled in a teaching degree at Bayfield.'

Ryan leaned back in his chair and studied the report again.

'Remarkable. She must have good family support. Even travelling for a couple of hours a day must be difficult.'

'Her father's principal of the local high school and her mother's a pre-primary teacher.' Tara smiled at the recollection of Pippa's stubbornness in her insistence she embark on a career in teaching. Tara suspected teaching was in her blood, and she had encouraged the young woman to pursue her dream by example. Nothing was impossible if you wanted it enough. 'Her father has organised for a lot of her coursework to be done online, so she only has to travel one or two days a week. The last six months, when the rheumatoid has been really active, she's resorted to using a wheelchair a few times.'

'A wheelchair?' Ryan's eyebrows elevated.

Tara nodded. 'Only as a last resort. She's really tried hard to overcome her condition, and considering her age—'

'She has her whole life ahead of her.'

'Exactly.' Tara fiddled with the hem of her blouse for a moment, suddenly overcome with emotion at the thought of what Pippa had gone through and the future that lay ahead. 'Do you think a hip replacement is an option?'

'Without seeing her, my thoughts are that surgical treatment would be effective in getting rid of her pain, and would probably restore mobility to the joint…'

'But?'

Tara could tell he had doubts.

'But she's so young. Even with the latest prosthesis, and the possibility of replacing the joint without cement, she'd be lucky to get twenty years out of a new joint. The best scenario would be that she'd be in her forties and need surgery again.'

Tara hesitated before voicing her own thoughts.

'Twenty years without pain is better than twenty years of agony. That's my personal opinion.'

Tara's simple statement cut to Ryan's core, and the few moments' silence seemed to stretch way too long. Her face was serious and Ryan tried to read her thoughts.

Was she talking, just a little, about herself?

Eventually he spoke.

'She's a little like you, isn't she?'

Tara fidgeted, and then looked up straight into his eyes with poignant honesty. She cleared her throat.

'Maybe a bit.'

'Was I part of your pain?'

Ryan could see the pulse in her neck and it was accelerating.

'I don't understand what you mean?'

He decided to be brutally direct. There were still things about the accident and the aftermath he didn't understand.

'Removing me from your life lessened your pain, helped you cope?'

'In a way,' Tara said in barely more than a whisper. 'I'd lost so much... Having to deal with your distress and uncertainty as well as my own was just as bad as the somatic pain of my injuries. Can you understand that?'

Ryan nodded, swallowing the lump that had lodged in his throat.

She continued. 'I'm sorry if I hurt you, but it was for a reason. In some ways the divorce was a relief. The last thing I wanted was for you to stay with me out of guilt or duty.' She looked away. 'And I believed you'd stopped loving me, despite your insistence that you'd do anything for me. I was scared witless of messing up *both* our lives.'

Her eyes were moist but Ryan needed to know.

'Do you still think that? That I stopped loving you?'

Tara took a deep breath and continued to fix her gaze on the window.

'I…I don't know. It's been eight years. Some of my memories are blurred. We're both different people with completely different lives compared with back then. It was a shock to see you again. You remarried. You have a child. And I'm coping in the best way I can—better than that, I am succeeding. If we'd stayed together there was no way of predicting if we'd be happy over the long term. I felt the odds were stacked against us.' She paused. 'I'm happy with my life now.'

'Are you?'

'Of course I am.'

'How did you feel about me marrying again?' He hesitated. 'I couldn't commit to a new relationship for a long time. It was over three years after we split before I met Shannay.' The question was blunt but Tara didn't have to answer if it was too painful.

She swung her gaze back to him and said with purpose, 'I was pleased. It's what I wanted—for you to find someone else who could provide the happiness that I couldn't. Someone who could give you the children you always wanted—'

'The children *we* always wanted.'

She looked away.

'That I could no longer provide.'

Ryan knew that wasn't strictly true, but he wasn't about to start an argument.

'I never loved Shannay.'

'Why did you marry her, then?'

'I thought I loved her. She was beautiful and charismatic and young. Too young, really. I was still grieving over the accident and losing you. I know that now. Shannay and I weren't compatible. She got bored with me and she was the one who wanted us to separate.'

'But what about your daughter? Shannay must love her.'

'Of course she does. But I sometimes think Shannay's too...er...flighty to be a good mother.'

Tara looked truly devastated, and Ryan realised he'd said the wrong thing. He remembered how passionate Tara had been about having children. She'd sworn she'd not make the same mistakes as her parents. And he'd believed it could have worked. It wouldn't have been easy, but if the passion had been there they could have at least tried. He now had a greater understanding of Tara's reasons for wanting him out of her life at such a momentously traumatic time. It made him want to be there for her now.

And he'd *never* fallen out of love with her.

Tara rubbed her hands nervously across her thighs.

'There's something I need to know, Ryan.'

He remained silent while Tara appeared to be summoning up the courage to go on. She had the hint of tears in her eyes, but bravely fought them back. She swallowed.

'Why are you here, Ryan? I don't understand. Why have you chosen to work in Keysdale when you hate the country and with your qualifications and experience could have just about any job for which you applied? To me, opening old wounds serves no purpose, and if you simply wanted to reassure yourself that *my* life wasn't in tatters, and you had absolutely no cause to be guilty, a visit or two would have sufficed.' She sucked in a breath and clenched her hands together in her lap. 'Why, Ryan? Why have you done this to me?'

Tara's poignant and emotive outburst had a similar effect to being hit in the guts with a sledgehammer. She thought he had a hidden agenda—which was the last thing he would have dumped on her. He needed to salvage his credibility.

'I… I…' But he battled to find the right words. Tara's tearful gaze didn't help. 'I couldn't really refuse—'

'I don't believe that for a minute.' Tara's distress had morphed into a look of steely determination. The only answer she would accept would be the truth.

'Just listen for a minute.'

'Go on.' Tara nodded.

'I've only worked for Southern Orthopaedics for just over a year. Before that I was in New Zealand for six months in a specialised lower limb unit. I'm literally the new kid on the block, and I have what the senior partners consider minimal family commitments. It's almost a rite of passage for a junior consultant to spend time overseas and be seconded to a rural practice. If you refuse you tend to stagnate and you are not considered for the more…er… esteemed—'

'You mean promotions.' Tara interrupted. She had been listening intently and seemed to believe him. 'And the position in Keysdale just happened to come up?'

'The past…our history…it was purely coincidence…'

With a decent lashing of fate.

Tara's hands relaxed and she rubbed one forearm with her other hand.

'You've never been good at lying, Ryan, so I doubt you'd have made it up.' She gathered together Pippa Morgan's notes. 'I believe you.'

She began to lift herself on to her wheelchair.

'It's time for me to go home.'

She looked tired and stifled a yawn.

'Can we at least be friends?' Ryan said with apprehension. He had no idea whether he had gained any ground with Tara.

She looked at him with a penetrating gaze but said nothing.

'Right, then. I'll help you put the chair into the car.'

Tara positioned herself comfortably in the driver's seat and as soon as Ryan had loaded the chair reversed and set off down the road at a speed just short of burning rubber. On the way she glimpsed the local mechanic's van and the old wreck the garage staff used for pick-ups and deliveries heading for the Riverside. Ryan's hire car, no doubt. She chuckled. But it wasn't her problem.

The return of her ex-husband into her life was, though. No matter how hard she tried she couldn't clear him from her thoughts.

Removing the man she'd once loved from her life had been a major contribution to deadening the emotional pain resulting from the loss of many of the things that had been important to her—her physical strength and agility, her independence, *her attractiveness.* The biggest blow, though, had been to her self-esteem.

Now Ryan was back he'd rekindled some of those feelings that belonged in the past. Feelings that went deeper than a platonic friendship, than simple physical attraction. She felt the same intimate connection they'd shared before the accident—the ability to know what the other was thinking, the desire to comfort when the other was hurting, the yearning for mutual happiness and the sharing of goals in a future that stretched *until death us do part.*

Was that love?

It wasn't worth even trying to answer the question. Even if it was, loving Ryan again would almost certainly mean more pain. There were too many reasons why the relationship wouldn't...*couldn't* work. Geography, lifestyle and a small child who had probably had more disruption in her life than most adults.

She wished she could believe the old saying that *love conquers all*, but she had a feeling a future with Ryan now would be more likely to fail than eight years ago. Both she and Ryan had new and different lives, and it was dangerous to even think about taking risks.

She'd just have to work harder at making sure her heart was impenetrable.

There was no point in falling for this intelligent, charming, sensitive man all over again even though she could feel it happening. An attraction based on the past could only lead to disaster. She had to nip her feelings in the bud before they began to blossom.

Tara was surprised her mother and father didn't come out to meet her, so she honked her horn twice—the signal she used to alert them she was home. A few minutes later Jane appeared in the doorway, a worried expression on her face, and Tara prepared herself for the inevitable grilling.

'Thank God you're home,' Jane said as she opened the car door. It certainly wasn't the greeting Tara was expecting. Had something happened? Some bad news?

'What's the matter, Mum?'

'It's your father. He's had an accident and he's refusing to go to the hospital.'

Tara's heart began to thud irregularly, and she felt the blood drain from her face, but the light-headedness only lasted a few seconds. It was at times like this she missed being able to leap out of the car and run inside. The wait for her mother to get her chair so she could go in and see for herself what had happened was an agony of uncertainty.

'What happened?' She couldn't help the impatient note in her voice.

'Darby was in one of his bad moods,' Tara's mother said breathlessly as she wheeled the chair from the back, not bothering to close the door. 'And today your father wasn't quick enough to get out of the way. He's got a chunk out of his leg, and I think he's either badly sprained or broken his wrist.'

Tara processed the information as she lifted herself out of the car.

Darby, a now aging pony, had been a gift for Tara's eighth birthday and she had loved him to bits—still did. He'd probably been a substitute for the siblings she'd never had, and she'd treasured the solitary rides they'd shared when she'd chatter away to him and reveal her deepest secrets.

He'd been literally put out to pasture since Tara had stopped riding him, and was usually placid. Over the last six months or so he'd been prone to stubbornness and the occasional temper tantrum where he'd kick and try to buck. Tara had laughingly said he had equine Alzheimer's. She doubted he'd be capable of causing any major damage, though.

Her mother, casting worried looks in Tara's direction, led the way into the house and Tara followed her to the kitchen.

It took Tara only a few seconds to take in the blood-soaked towel on her father's shin and the roughly applied elastic bandage on his left wrist. Graham's expression was a mix of frustration, pain and anger.

'It's not as bad as it looks,' he said in an unusually quiet voice, doing his best to hide a grimace. 'Blasted horse,' he added, as if apportioning blame made it easier for him to cope.

'Let me have a look.' Tara wheeled over to where her father sat in a spindle-backed chair next to the kitchen table. 'Are you in a lot of pain?'

Tara could tell he was, but he was unlikely to

admit it. It was one of those crazy man things, to deny pain.

'Just a bit. Mainly in my leg,' he said through clenched teeth.

Tara carefully removed the towel from her father's leg and it took a great deal of effort to suppress her gasp.

A chunk of flesh the size of the palm of her hand had been torn away from his shin just below the knee, exposing bone and muscle. There was no deformity, so she hoped the bones were intact. Her mother had obviously cleaned the edges of the wound as best she could, but there were flecks of dirt and possibly manure embedded in the exposed area and a steady ooze of blood from one side of the wound. For his leg alone he needed X-rays, cleaning and debridement of the wound, a tetanus booster and antibiotics. There was a real possibility he would need a skin graft.

Tara took the clean towel her mother offered and covered the wound, instructing her to apply pressure while Tara began to unwind the bandage. To her relief, the skin of Graham's hand wasn't broken, and again there was no obvious deformity, but there was some swelling of his wrist.

'How did you do this?' she asked calmly.

Her father seemed to have succumbed to his fate and replied meekly, with what she thought was a hint of a smile on his face, 'I tried to give Darby the same as he gave me.'

Tara thought for a second.

'You mean you tried to kick an elderly pony that was having a temper tantrum?'

Her father nodded. Why didn't that surprise her?

'And I slipped,' he added.

'And landed on your outstretched hand?'

'Yeah, that's right.'

He winced as she prodded the dip in the back of his hand near the base of his thumb—over his scaphoid bone.

'That hurts?'

He nodded again.

'Anywhere else?'

He shrugged

She manipulated his wrist and asked him to flex and extend his fingers but couldn't find evidence of any other injuries.

'Dad, you're not going to like what I'm about to say, but Mum's right—you need to go to hospital, and you might even need surgery. That wound on your leg is deep, and you've almost certainly done some damage to at least one of the small bones in your hand.'

Her father scowled but seemed accepting.

'Tonight?' he grumbled.

'The sooner the better.'

Tara's father, not surprisingly, refused her suggestion they call an ambulance. By the time she'd phoned the hospital, organised Rob Whelan—the on-call doctor covering emergencies—to meet them in the small ED of the local community hospital and supervised her father's transfer from house to car, it was nearly ten o'clock. Graham tried to manage the short walk to Tara's car unassisted, and even using Jane on one side and a broom on the other as a crutch she could tell he was in a great deal of pain. He'd definitely need a wheelchair when they arrived at Keysdale.

With her father in the back seat, her mother driving and Tara settled in the passenger side they set off.

Tara glanced behind her and noticed her father had his eyes closed but was still grimacing. He'd refused to take anything for the pain, which was just as well as it was likely he'd need surgery—if only to clean and debride his wound. If that was the case he'd need a drip, and analgesia could be given through the vein. Fortunately Rob could do a simple debridement, but if Graham needed more complicated surgery he'd have to be transferred to the regional hospital in Bayfield. She wasn't looking forward to his reaction, even if his injuries turned out to be minor.

'Nearly there,' her mother said, attempting cheerfulness. They turned off Hill Park Road onto the highway heading towards the town.

Her father groaned as they jolted over a pothole.

'Sorry,' Jane said. 'I didn't see it.'

Graham's silence was an ominous sign that indicated he either didn't have the energy or was too focused on his injuries to complain.

They pulled up to the front of the hospital and parked in the area designated for ambulances. Laurie, the night orderly, and Kath, one of the ED nurses, stood waiting with both a gurney and a wheelchair. Graham had obviously noticed.

'I don't need those things. I'm quite capable of getting inside under my own steam.'

'Like you were at home?' Jane was quick to reply, the strain showing in her voice and on her face.

Graham attempted to move his leg and this time

the movement was accompanied by a string of expletives.

Laurie brought the chair next to the car and then glanced at Tara. 'Is this okay to transport your father, Dr Fielding?'

At that moment Rob Whelan arrived, leaped out of his car and strode towards them. To Tara's relief, after acknowledging her and her mother's presence, he took over with an assertiveness that defied protest.

While Graham was carefully moved to the wheelchair without the clamour of expected complaints, Jane brought Tara's chair from the back of the car and stood by while she transferred. Once Tara was in her chair she noticed her mother had begun to tremble. Reaching out, she gave her hand a squeeze.

'He'll be all right, Mum. You know he's in good hands.'

Jane took a deep breath and her hands steadied. 'I know that, love.'

'Why don't you go inside and I'll lock up the car?'

'But—'

'Just go and be with Dad. He needs you.'

In the five minutes or so it took Tara to make her way inside to the Emergency Room, Graham had been undressed, his grubby clothes replaced by a hospital gown, and Kath was opening a dressing pack. The blood-soaked towel had been replaced by a large sterile pad of gauze, and Rob Whelan was busy inserting an IV. He glanced at Tara.

'I've done a lightning examination, but he needs analgesia and the quickest way is into the vein.' Then he smiled. 'But of course I don't have to tell you that.'

'No, but I'm sure Mum and Dad would appreciate you explaining things in layman's terms.' Tara resisted the temptation to quiz her colleague about the seriousness of her father's injuries as he'd probably barely had time to take a history and would no doubt do a more thorough examination once the pain had eased.

Jane stood silently on the other side of the couch, looking pale and tired. She'd most likely put up with at least an hour of Graham's undiluted anger while they waited for Tara to arrive home.

'Of course.' But Rob's conversation was still directed to Tara. 'I've asked Meg to phone the radiographer.' He lowered his voice. 'I suspect he's cracked his tibia and almost certainly has a fractured scaphoid.' He cleared his throat. 'And Meg's also going to see if she can contact Ryan Dennison.

He has a short list tomorrow, so I assume he's still in town.'

'No! I don't want that man touching me!' Graham said in a loud, angry voice.

Four pairs of eyes fixed on him, but Tara's were the only ones wide with horror at the realisation of how deep her father's dislike of Ryan was, even after all these years. Rob looked stunned. He had no idea. He'd taken the helm of the practice nearly five years ago, when old Doc Harris retired. Rob was a relative newcomer and had no knowledge of her history with Ryan.

'Why? You know Dr Dennison?' Rob said.

Graham scowled.

'I thought I did.'

Tara felt the heat of her father's stare as his gaze shifted to her and fixed on her legs.

'Before he crippled my daughter.'

CHAPTER FOUR

THE main reason Ryan couldn't sleep was because it was so quiet. His city residence, a second-floor apartment in South Perth, was on a busy street, and he hadn't realised background noise was his default setting. In his restless state of insomnia, his thoughts were only of Tara.

What a determined, courageous woman she was. Despite the limitations imposed by her paraplegia, she'd not let it hold her back and had embraced life with an enthusiasm he admired. But he doubted she had much in the way of positive feelings for him. When he'd asked her if she still believed he'd stopped loving her, she'd been vague and skirted around the issue. Their love had been shattered to pieces in a few seconds in which his reflex response had been the wrong one…and he could never put it right.

But he did still love her.

He flung the quilt off the bed and pulled the sheet up to his waist in an effort to get comfortable enough to entice sleep. It made little difference. In the deathly silence of the outskirts of a country town at eleven on a Friday night he was yearning for at least a little traffic noise.

So it was almost a relief when his mobile phone rang.

'Ryan Dennison,' he said, not recognising the number of the caller.

'Hello, Dr Dennison. It's Meg Davies, a casualty sister at the hospital. I'm sorry to disturb you so late.'

'The hospital? I'm sorry, which hospital?'

'Keysdale.'

'Oh. What can I do for you?'

It hadn't been written into his job description that he covered orthopaedic emergencies after hours, but Rob Whelan had negotiated an agreement that he would attend emergency patients during the two or three days a week he visited the town.

'You'd be lucky to be called out at night more than once a month, and major trauma cases go directly to Bayfield,' Rob had said jovially while he was filling out the paperwork granting him admitting rights to Keysdale hospital.

Tonight was only his second day working in the town. His so-called operating session the previous day had been an orientation day, where he'd met some of the hospital staff and been shown the facilities; he had no post-operative inpatients. The call was most likely an emergency.

He heard the nurse clear her throat and what sounded like raised voices in the background.

'We have a patient here Dr Whelan was hoping you could come in and see.'

'Okay, can you fill me in with a brief summary?'

There were more noises in the background, muffled as if the nurse had covered the handpiece of the phone.

'Dr Fielding wants to talk to you. She'll be able to explain better than I.'

Tara?

What on earth was she doing at the hospital at this hour of night? He had a fleeting thought that she was the patient, that she'd been injured. He was usually calm in times of crisis but he felt the effects of adrenaline surging through his circulation.

'Hello, Ryan, it's Tara.'

Ryan exhaled a breath that had somehow caught in his throat.

'What's happened? Why are you at the hospital?'

She hesitated a moment before replying, as if she

needed time to formulate what she was about to say. Almost as if she was going to impart bad news.

'It's Dad. He had an altercation with Darby, my old pony. Rob's just got the X-rays back and he has an undisplaced open crack fracture to his right tibia. He also has a scaphoid fracture, and the radiographer says there's at least two millimetres displacement.'

She sounded understandably anxious, her voice high and staccato.

'I'll come straight over. I should be able to get there in about ten minutes.'

'No, Ryan. There's a problem. If you could just give some advice over the phone…'

'A problem? What problem?'

'Er…Dad's creating a bit of a fuss. He refuses point-blank to see you.'

Ryan took a moment to take in what Tara had just told him. It made sense. Not only did Graham dislike him, he obviously nursed a deep mistrust of his one-time son-in-law. It was unfortunate that lack of trust extended to include Ryan's professional skills. But he wasn't about to let a strong-willed, one-eyed farmer put him off.

'Like I said, I'll be there in ten minutes and we can sort Graham's issues when I get there.'

After he ended the call, without giving Tara time to reply, he felt a little guilty. But he needed to see the X-rays to know if Graham required surgery. If that was the case, the ideal situation would be to put him on the end of his operation list the following day. At worst it would simply mean referral to a surgeon in the nearest regional centre.

He pulled on the jeans and tee shirt he'd been wearing earlier, travelled the two strides to the bathroom and splashed cold water on his face. Finger-combing the spikes from his tousled hair, he grabbed his medical bag, slipped into his shoes and headed out to… He suddenly remembered that his mode of transport, delivered not long after Tara had left, was a battered, noisy work ute lent to him by the mechanic because neither of the two Keysdale vehicle rentals was available until the following day—by which time he'd been assured his own car would be back on the road.

After a clunky gear-change he rumbled off, and ten minutes later was pressing the after-hours buzzer at the entrance to the ED of the hospital.

'You stay with Dad,' Tara said with a weary sigh.

Ryan was busy writing up Graham's notes and reorganising his theatre list. He'd been a prince of patience and reason, the way he'd calmly explained the different options available to the stubborn farmer. The threat of sending Tara's father to Bayfield and the possibility of having long-term problems with his hand and wrist if the scaphoid fracture wasn't fixed promptly had won out. Fortunately Jane's attitude to Ryan was less hostile, but the seeds of blame and guilt were still embedded in her heart, and Tara knew the relationship her parents had with her ex-husband would never be the same.

'But—' Jane croaked in a voice laced with tiredness.

'No buts, Mum. I'm quite capable of getting into Ryan's car. He can leave my chair in the car and I'll use the manual one when we get home. I've got a spare key so Ryan can move it away from the ambulance entry.'

Tara's gaze shifted from Jane to her father, who was snoring softly, no doubt due to the effects of the morphine that was coursing through his veins. If he'd been aware of the arrangements she was making for Ryan to drive her home he'd have blown his stack, but thankfully he was peacefully sleeping.

Her mother looked too tired to protest, but it had

been her choice to stay with her husband at least until he was settled in the ward.

'Oh, all right.' She suppressed a yawn. But then she was suddenly wide awake, with a panicked look on her face.

'What, Mum? What's the matter?'

'Milking…the herd…I'll have to come home. The cows aren't going to wait.'

She began gathering her things.

It took seconds for Tara to realise that the problems the Fielding family were about to face didn't only involve Graham. And it took her less than a minute to formulate a plan—a plan she would have considered totally out of the question if she hadn't spent the evening with Ryan. She had a gut feeling he would help without her having to ask him. After all she'd used to know him with an intimacy that was only present in a committed couple who were deeply in love.

She placed her hand on her mother's trembling arm and felt the tension in Jane's muscles, strung taut like new fencing wire.

'Mum.' Tara's voice was steady, with a tone she hoped conveyed control. Her mother relaxed only a fraction, and the look of dread in her eyes conveyed more than mere words. 'Forget about the farm. What do you really want to do?'

Her mother opened her mouth to speak but the words seemed to stick in her throat.

'I can't forget about the farm,' she finally said, withdrawing her arm from Tara's hold and gathering up her handbag. She fumbled with the zip, and when she finally opened the bag she couldn't find what she was looking for. It was the last straw. She began sobbing.

Tara leaned across and drew her mother close at the same time as Ryan quietly slipped into the cubicle. He didn't speak, but his presence was oddly reassuring.

'*I* can manage,' Tara said softly, with a conviction that defied argument.

She paused, waiting for her mother's response. But Jane said nothing, as if making decisions was too much for her after such a long and stressful day.

Tara glanced briefly at Ryan. 'And Ryan can help me with the few things I can't do on my own. It will only be for the morning milking. Tomorrow I'll be able to organise some local help.'

She heard Ryan catch his breath but he gave nothing away. He didn't show any signs of surprise, or confusion, or incredulity—the emotions he was probably experiencing as a result of her sudden, unexpected request. It was as if she'd simply asked him to make her a cup of tea. He nodded his agreement.

'So, what do you *really* want to do, Mum?' Tara repeated.

Jane pulled away and took a deep, sighing breath.

'I want to be with your father.'

'Right, that's settled, then. I'll see you tomorrow—and *don't worry about the milking.*'

Tara kissed her mother on the cheek before she reversed out of the cubicle, raising her hand in a wave. Meg was at her desk but she stood when she saw Tara and Ryan.

'We're ready to take your father to the ward.' A look of concern crossed her face. 'Are you going to be able to manage on your own?'

She wasn't on her own, though. For better or worse, she'd roped Ryan into the latest Fielding family drama and it was too late to bail out. She needed him. The thought was scary, and strangely exciting at the same time.

'Yes, I'll be fine. Dr Dennison is going to help out.'

There was no mistaking the meaning behind Meg's quizzical look and the momentary upward twitch of her eyebrows. Tara suspected several versions of the news of the favour Dr Ryan Dennison was granting her in the small hours of Saturday morning would be all over town by the end of the weekend.

But there was nothing she could do to stop it.

Ryan wasn't sure what he'd let himself in for when he'd agreed to Tara's request to take her back to the farm and help with the milking. If she'd asked him to speak at a conference, or organise a meeting with the local politician, or even charm his way into a late booking at his favourite waterside restaurant in the city, he'd be in his element. He'd been raised in the Big Smoke and knew the drill.

He didn't actually hate the country...or farming... or getting dirt and sweat on his freshly laundered clothes. He thought of his attitude as being more like a fear of the unknown. In fact he could use exactly the same phrase to describe his feelings towards Tara at the moment.

Fear?

He couldn't get rid of the anxiety niggling at the edge of his usual calm demeanour—and, yes, he was a little frightened of being alone for the rest of the night with Tara. It was all to do with the fact he'd used to know this woman intimately. And earlier tonight she'd been frank with him to the point where she had come close to opening her heart.

He needed time to think through his next move with her. She wasn't a stranger, but he had to get to know this new Tara Fielding all over again. He had the feeling it would take more than charm for Tara to allow him into her present-day world. And he wanted to do it when *she* was ready.

They made their way to the ute.

'Sorry about the transport. It was all Keysdale had to offer at short notice.' Ryan doubted she'd complain. She'd been raised on a working farm after all.

'No problem.' She stopped on the passenger side, waiting for him to open the door.

'Once I'm in, you'll remember how to strap my chair onto the hoist and park it in my car, won't you?'

'Yes, I'm pretty sure I can manage.'

She held out a bunch of keys, singling out the car key. 'And if you wouldn't mind shifting the car into the car park. The hand controls don't interfere with using the floor pedals. You just drive it like a normal car.'

'Oh, okay.'

He seemed to be learning new things about Tara and her lifestyle at a rate of knots that he was battling to keep up with. He wondered how she had learned to cope all those years ago, when she'd been so resistant to his many offers of help. Back then he'd not had the strength to stand firm. He'd been a prisoner in his own guilt-ridden anguish and had succumbed to Tara's wishes without more than a token protest. Now he wished he'd been more persistent. Trying to contact her without being confrontational by phone and e-mail in the first couple of years after the divorce hadn't been enough. He should have put aside his fear of having to deal with Graham's and Jane's anger as well as another rejection from Tara and forced her to talk to him. Doubts surfaced. He wondered if it was too late to start all over again? But his circumstances were different—he had a child to cope with now.

He opened the borrowed vehicle and went to reach across his companion to open the door, but she beat him to it. In what he guessed were less than a couple of minutes she'd shifted from her chair to the dusty, work-battered seat and was in the process of buckling her seatbelt. He paused to admire her and she looked up with a nervous smile.

'What's up? Is everything okay?'

'Yes, fine.' He certainly wasn't about to tell her that everything was far from being okay. That his mind was becoming increasingly scrambled with feelings he didn't understand. And it had nothing to do with the tiredness that hung heavy like early-morning mist. He fumbled to release the brake on her chair and finally managed to move it to Tara's vehicle.

'You remember the way home, don't you?' Tara asked as he positioned himself behind the wheel.

Home? Of course *her* home was the farm, and had been since her discharge from the rehabilitation hospital. That had been several months after their divorce and was a part of her life he knew nothing about.

He remembered when *home* had been a shabby two-bedroom flat near the university that he and Tara had shared with another couple who were also struggling students. He recalled the excitement when they'd moved into a smart townhouse by the river after they were married, and the joy they'd shared in choosing furniture, in packing the small courtyard garden haphazardly with dozens of plants, and filling their lives with dreams and plans for a future—a future that had been cruelly stolen from them.

'You *do* remember the way to the farm?' she repeated.

Ryan had been so swept up in his own thoughts he'd not answered.

'Yes, of course,' he said, a little more brusquely than he'd planned, and his terse response put an end to their conversation until he turned onto the gravel road leading to the homestead. 'I made my own way here a few weeks ago, didn't I?'

He pulled up as close as he could to the ramp without getting in Tara's way, and was grateful someone had had the forethought to leave an outside light on. There were also several rooms bathed in a welcoming golden glow.

Tara was again handing him her keys. This time she'd separated a brass door key from the rest.

'My other wheelchair is in my bedroom. Do you remember where that is?'

Of course he did. How could he forget those stolen moments of tantalising intimacy on the few occasions they'd visited the farm when they'd been students, uninhibited with their affections and so much in love.

'Vaguely.'

He had a sudden idea, and the words were out of

his mouth before he had time to think of the implications.

'Look, why don't I just carry you inside? If you need the chair I can find it when you're settled.' He paused, waiting for her reply, but it didn't happen. Her face was in shadow, so he couldn't see her expression. He figured he had nothing to lose. She hadn't agreed, but she also hadn't refused. 'And I don't mind putting you to bed. It's been a long day and I'm feeling dead on my feet.'

Dead on my feet...

How insensitive was that?

Tara turned towards him and he could now see the icy look on her face, the steely defiance in her eyes. He'd hit a raw nerve and he braced himself for the consequences.

'I'm not a child, Ryan,' she said quietly. 'I don't want to be carried, let alone put to bed like a helpless baby. I'm quite capable of putting myself to bed, on my own, just like I've been doing for the past eight years.'

Despite the gloom Ryan could see her red cheeks and the veins standing out on her temples. He suspected her rosy complexion was more to do with anger than embarrassment.

His heart filled with regret. He certainly hadn't planned to hurt her.

'I'm sorry, Tara. I didn't think…' he said meekly. He took the offered key and climbed out of his car. 'I won't be long,' he added as he strode towards the house, wondering how he could have got it so wrong.

Tara had become used to her predictable life with its strictly regimented routine. That wasn't to say she was completely happy with it, but at least she knew there would be few surprises.

The first shock had been Ryan appearing on her doorstep and telling her he was about to edge his way back into a part of her life she'd thought she had control of. Then, even scarier, had come the revelation he was divorced with a child, and that information was all tangled up with the realisation she still found her ex-husband attractive. Up until now she hadn't believed that to be a problem, because all she had to do was have as little contact with him as possible.

But now!

She'd shared a meal with him at his motel, he was the treating specialist for her stubborn and hostile father, and he was about to spend what was left of the night with her.

Oh, God.

Her privacy, her independence, her fragile self-confidence was crumbling around her.

She was grateful Ryan had gone inside to get her wheelchair as it gave her a few moments to rein back her emotions and think about how she was going to handle the next five or six hours. Had she been too harsh with him when he'd offered to carry her inside?

Carry her!

She wasn't ready for that kind of close physical contact and didn't trust how her body would respond to being cradled in his arms. Better she just keep her distance—both physical and emotional. Ryan would be heading back to the city after his operating session and then they'd be in a better position to know how long her father would be out of action. The crisis at the farm would be over, or at least reduced to a manageable drama by the end of the weekend. She looked forward to some semblance of normality being restored.

Her thoughts were interrupted by a knock on the window. Ryan stood sheepishly behind her chair. She opened the car door. 'I'm sorry—'

'There's no need to apologise.' He had a tentative smile on his face, as if waiting for permission to go on. 'You're tired and have had an incredibly stressful night. I understand.'

Tara's first reaction was to recoil from words that could be interpreted as condescending. But he was right. Stressed and tired was exactly how she felt. Add a handful of guilt at not being home for her parents when her father had been injured, and it wasn't surprising her judgement was skewed.

'That still doesn't excuse my…er…grouchiness.'

His smile morphed into a grin.

'You always had a quick temper.' He paused and rubbed his forehead. 'But it never lasted for long. And I like a woman with spirit.'

'Enough,' she said quietly, feeling the edginess coming back. Ryan seemed to understand, and busied himself with positioning the chair as close to the car as he could.

She pulled herself into her chair and headed towards the open front door of the house, leaving Ryan to lock up the ute and follow her. The first thing she did when she got inside was to check there was fresh linen in the guest room. She also glanced in the bathroom and noted there were towels, fresh soap and a new toothbrush. She gave a silent cheer for her mother's efficiency, and as she turned to come out of the room nearly bumped into Ryan.

'Whoops,' he said as he moved aside. 'I just seem to keep getting in your way.'

She ignored his comment and stifled a yawn. 'We should try to get a few hours' sleep. I'll set my alarm for five, because we need to be in the milking shed by six at the latest. What time does your theatre session start?'

'Half past eight.'

The yawn she'd tried to suppress a minute ago returned but she ignored it.

'Good. If you're a fast learner...' which she doubted—he'd always shied away from any manual work involving more energy than moving the occasional plant pot '...you might have time to grab a bite to eat before you go back to the hospital.'

She thought of apologising for volunteering him for pre-dawn hard labour, but she was too tired and would think about an appropriate way to thank him in the morning. He obviously hadn't missed her yawn, and she harboured the thought that she didn't look her best after a long hard day, let alone one which had turned into an even longer and demanding night.

'To bed, then.' A cheeky smile appeared on his face and he added, 'You must be exhausted.'

'I think you're familiar with the guest room,' Tara muttered. and waved her arm in the direction of the room they'd just left. 'You should have everything you need—feel free to raid the kitchen if you're hungry.'

'Thanks.' They both hesitated, Ryan appearing as uncomfortable as Tara felt. 'I'll see you in the morning.'

He started off towards his room, but then stopped and turned. Two strides and he was back at Tara's side, and before she had time to stop him he'd leaned over and planted a warm, firm kiss on her lips.

Ryan had kissed her!

It was brief enough to be simply a goodnight kiss between friends but long enough to hold the promise of more… If she wanted it.

Did she? But Ryan didn't give her the opportunity to decide.

'Sweet dreams,' he said as he closed his door.

When Tara finally fell into a restless sleep she dreamed of Ryan's arms around her, his mouth on hers, his lips caressing. It was the sweetest dream—until he began to undress her and saw her injured legs. Then the sweetness evaporated and all she was left with was the same empty loneliness she'd endured for the last eight years.

CHAPTER FIVE

WHEN the loud buzz of Tara's alarm jolted her into consciousness the following morning it felt as if she'd only just gone to sleep. She stretched, rubbed her eyes and looked at the clock on her bedside table. Yes, it *was* just after five a.m. Time to get up. Her mother's words echoed in her mind—*the cows aren't going to wait.*

By the time she'd hauled herself out of bed, washed and attended to her usual morning ablutions, it was close to half past and she hoped Ryan wasn't still a heavy sleeper. When she knocked on his door he opened it with a wide-awake, cheerful smile. He'd obviously showered as he was towelling his still-damp hair and droplets of water trickled down his chest.

His bare, lean, muscular chest.

The noise that involuntarily emitted from Tara's suddenly tight throat was a cross between a moan and a gasp. All he wore was a pair of navy boxer shorts and a mischievous grin.

'It's not as if you haven't seen it all before.' He discarded the towel and pulled on jeans and a shirt.

By this time Tara's cheeks were burning, but she couldn't bring herself to look away. Memories flooded back. Bittersweet memories of carefree times when she'd felt no embarrassment over nakedness—hers or Ryan's. Back then she'd been comfortable with her body. She'd revelled in the sensuousness of just looking at Ryan naked; in the warm pleasure of unexpected arousal and lovemaking—in the shower, on the floor, leaned up against the front door, breathless and impatient, or lazily in bed on Sunday mornings.

But now? The thought of revealing her damaged body to Ryan—or any man—made her stomach turn.

Another blow to her fragile self esteem.

And why should Ryan be any different? A feral thought entered her mind associated with a vivid image of a very young, very energetic, nubile and sexy Shannay. The other ex-wife, who seemed much more real now she had a name. How could she compete with that?

'I wasn't expecting you to be awake.' She managed to salvage a morsel of control.

'You said we had an appointment at six with a

herd of impatient cows. I don't want to keep the ladies waiting.'

He then had the audacity to wink. He was flirting with her. *And she liked it.*

She glanced at his bare feet in an effort to take her mind off the rest of his body.

'There'll be a pair of spare wellies in the dairy and I'll lend you some thick socks,' she said. His designer running shoes would be ruined within five minutes in the milking shed.

'Thanks.' He slipped on his shoes without bothering with socks. 'Anything else we need to do before we go?'

'I'll need a couple of cushions—'

'So you can relax and watch me do all the work?' He laughed and, surprisingly, seemed to be enjoying the novelty of helping out.

She didn't want to burst the bubble and tell him he was in for at least an hour of unremitting hard toil. Tara ignored his remark as she reversed out of the doorway, Ryan not far behind. She did a quick detour to get the socks and cushions, which she piled on her lap.

'I'll take the quad bike. It's parked in the tractor shed. Then if you could put my chair in the truck...' She grabbed a set of keys from a hook near the back door and threw them at Ryan, who caught them clumsily. 'Then follow me to the dairy.'

There was something exhilarating about driving an old, beat-up farm truck along a potholed dirt track in the milky pre-dawn light. Ryan could make out the silhouettes of scattered trees on the blurry horizon, and he inhaled the heady smell of livestock and wet grass while he battled to keep up with the jolting tail-lights glowing just ahead.

He followed Tara around a broad bend, and in the sweep of his headlights witnessed an amazing sight.

The rising sun back-lit the dairy shed and bathed it in a golden glow. Behind the shed the ground in the paddock sloped up to a backdrop of gently rolling hills. In the distance he could see an army of cattle making their way towards them, a small brown dog running from one side of the herd to the other.

He parked the truck next to Tara, and as the cows moved closer he was embraced by the noise of them clomping and mooing in the otherwise quiet dawn. He glanced at his watch. Five forty-five. They'd arrived in good time.

Tara looked impatient to get started, so he lifted her chair out of the tray of the truck, unfolded it, positioned what seemed like a mountain of cushions on the seat and wheeled it over to the quad bike.

'If you could just help me onto the cushions?' she said.

Once she was on her chair, the cushions added an extra twenty centimetres to her height and when she turned the lights on in the dairy he understood why.

All the equipment, as well as the cattle stalls, was raised nearly a metre above ground level—he presumed so that the farmer and his helpers didn't have to constantly bend. Unfortunately the design didn't take into account the height disadvantage of a paraplegic worker. Hence the cushions.

'Why did you bring the bike?' Surely Tara could have just as easily travelled with him.

'Sometimes Jacko sleeps late—'

'Jacko?' he said. Who the hell was Jacko? Was Tara expecting hired help to arrive at any minute? A jolt of something very like jealousy surprised him.

Tara chuckled. 'The dog. Didn't you see him in the paddock when you pulled in?'

'Oh, yes, of course.' It made sense now. Farmers used motorbikes to round up stock. Tara used the quad bike if and when the energetic little Kelpie overslept—which he doubted happened very often.

After he was kitted out in wellies, rubber gloves,

a plastic apron and disposable cap, Ryan followed Tara into the shed. It was like entering a different world, full of stainless steel surfaces, machinery for milking, pipes seeming to go in all directions and a huge tank at the end of the run.

Tara seemed to know what she was doing, though.

'What can I do to help?' he said as she spun wheels, checked dials and wheeled up the work area that ran between the stalls where the cows would be milked.

'I've just done a flush of the system to clean it, and the cows will start coming through soon. Then it'll be non-stop.'

'Until we finish?'

'That's right. When one hundred and twenty-three cows are milked and back in the paddock.'

'You count them?'

'Every day. But it's done electronically nowadays. It's a way of keeping track of them. If they're not all accounted for it can mean trouble.'

She sighed, but Ryan could tell she was experiencing a buzz from being up to her ears in hard physical work. Somehow he couldn't imagine Graham Fielding letting Tara have free rein in the dairy, even if she'd been able-bodied. Her father had been protective of her all the years he and Tara had been together. It had been easy for her to move away to go to university, but the wheel had turned full circle.

He could only envisage what it must be like for her now, and had a new respect for how she was coping.

He felt her tugging at his sleeve and turned to see what she wanted. The cows were patiently waiting outside the shed so he assumed the milking was about to start.

'We'll take a side each. Your inexperience should balance with my being in the chair, so hopefully we'll synchronise.' She pointed to a gate on his side. 'Time to open up. I'll show you what to do with the first cow and then you're on your own.' She smiled. 'Watch closely, learn and then do it yourself, as my grandpa used to say.'

The next hour flew by in a blur of teats, milking cups, feed bins, cow excrement and noise. There wasn't time to talk even if Ryan had wanted to. Tara had been right—they got into a rhythm of sorts that they both could manage.

When the last half-dozen cows were released he felt as if he'd worked a twelve-hour shift moving rocks up a mountain. He'd discovered muscles he never knew he had and hoped he'd not have to use again any time soon. He stretched, wiped hot sweat from his throbbing forehead and groaned. Tara manoeuvred to face him.

'You did really well. I'm impressed. Especially since you always seemed to be glued to the city with orthopaedic cement.'

'Don't sound so surprised.' He detected a touch of sarcasm in her comments but chose to ignore it. All she did was shrug and reach her hand to massage a very attractively muscled shoulder. He wondered what it would be like to have her strong fingers kneading his own tender muscles. 'And I assumed this was a one-off. An emergency. I couldn't exactly refuse.'

The smile on her face disappeared, and Ryan wasn't sure if it was because he'd said the wrong thing, or because she was disappointed he wasn't planning on making a habit of early-morning milking.

'What now?'

'I'll clean and disinfect the tubing, if you could hose out the stalls.' She looked at her watch. 'And we might even have time for a quick breakfast.'

Tara decided to leave the bike at the dairy, saying she would get the dairyman to bring it back in the afternoon.

'The dairyman?' Ryan was curious. He'd assumed the Fielding family ran the farm single-handed. He squinted at the low morning sun, concentrating on negotiating potholes that seemed to have multiplied since he'd made the trip in the dark.

'We open the farm on the weekend to tourists, or to groups of schoolkids by appointment on week-days, so that they can see how a working dairy farm runs. One of the neighbour's boys comes over to help.'

Of course. Ryan remembered the leaflets he'd noticed at the motel. He stole a glance at his com-panion. She was coiling a tendril of hair between her restless fingers.

'Haven't your parents got enough to do—?'

'They have,' she interrupted tersely. 'It's to do with money—you know, making ends meet.'

So his suspicions were confirmed—they had been struggling. It made Graham's injuries all the more serious…and distressing. If he was out of ac-tion and they had to employ someone else it would make their situation even worse.

'I'm sorry. I didn't realise,' he finally said.

They travelled the rest of the short journey back to the farmhouse in silence. When they rounded the bend on the approach to the homestead they saw Tara's car parked out at the front.

'Mum's back,' Tara said, her brow furrowing in a frown. 'I only hope Dad's—'

But her words were interrupted by the sight of a tired but smiling Jane emerging from the front door. She waved and started down the steps as Ryan pulled up next to the car.

Tara opened the door and hugged her mother with a down-to-earth affection he'd never known from his own parents.

'How's Dad?' Tara asked as she sat back and sighed.

'As well as we can expect. At least he's accepted the wisdom of having surgery. The driving force is his getting back to work as soon as he can. He seemed to forget about the milking, though, thank goodness. I think his brain was a bit numbed by the morphine.' She paused and held her daughter at arm's length. 'So how did the milking go?' Then she glanced at Ryan and smiled, but without any sign of the affection she'd shown towards her daughter. 'Thank you so much for helping out.'

He returned her smile. 'My pleasure.' To his surprise he realised the words had a ring of truth. He had actually enjoyed the hour of gruelling hard labour with Tara.

'So how did it go?' Tara's mother repeated, her eyes still fixed on Ryan, almost challenging.

'You'd better ask your daughter.'

Tara was positioning herself, ready to climb out onto her chair.

'A bit slow, but we managed.'

It was hardly a compliment, but the circumstances had been difficult.

'Good. Have you two got time for some breakfast? I've got scrambled eggs ready to cook. It'll only take five minutes.'

Country hospitality obviously outweighed her reticence to accept Ryan and all the baggage he still carried involving the Fielding family. The thought of fresh-cooked eggs had Ryan's mouth watering, but he looked across at Tara to see if she approved.

'Have you got time?' she asked.

'I'll make time,' he said graciously as he climbed out of the truck and hoisted the wheelchair from the back.

'Good.' Jane turned to go back into the house and Ryan found himself alone with Tara again. He wheeled the chair to where she waited, but stopped a few feet away.

'What's the matter?' she said.

It was a simple question, but it was enough to unleash an unexpected flow of raw emotion in Ryan; as if a dam had burst. She looked so beautiful—a smudge of dirt smeared on her neck, her hair enchantingly dishevelled, clothes damp with sweat. She smelled of fresh milk, hay and wholesomeness.

But now was not the time to tell her *everything* was the matter. He wanted to hold her in his arms, kiss her senseless and love her…make love with her. But he knew his thoughts were pure fantasy. He'd had his chance and would have to work hard for a second one.

He hesitated.

'Nothing,' he replied.

And all he could do was look away into the distance. What hope did he have of making up for the traumas of the past?

Very little.

Freshly showered and with a full stomach, Ryan drove back towards Keysdale. He would be late starting his operating session but it couldn't be helped, and stressing about it wouldn't change things. None of the three cases were emergencies, and half an hour either way wouldn't make any difference.

Huh?

Stressing about it wouldn't change things?

Normally stress was his driving force, but his stress meter had been reset and he felt unusually calm. Pretty damned tired as well, but calm and alert and surprisingly content with the world. The physiological reason was probably to do with the release of endorphins, the body's happy hormones, after a morning that could be compared to a full-on, two-hour gym workout, or running the City to Surf, or… No, he wouldn't go there. There was no point in going back to that long-ago place and time when a night of lovemaking with Tara would leave them both breathless and exhausted but somehow renewed.

He eased his foot onto the brake, slowing down as he approached the intersection of Hill Park Road and the highway. A long-haul, fully loaded prime mover sped by in a cloud of gravel dust as its inside wheels skimmed the road shoulder. It wavered for a moment before finding the blacktop and its stability again.

In an odd way that was exactly how Ryan felt—wavering close to something precariously dangerous, with an outcome that could go either way. He could play it safe, drive slowly, not take any risks and maintain a professional but friendly distance from Tara. Or he could put his foot down on the accelerator, follow his heart and steamroll into something he had no control over that could easily end in disaster.

The second option was definitely risky, the first not worth considering. He would just have to look for a middle road. Yes, that was what he would do. Try and get to know Tara again and to understand her life, with its challenges and successes. But it would be up to her. She was the only one who could decide whether to let him into her life again.

And if she said no?

Well, he'd deal with that when it happened.

The effect of the happy hormones was beginning to wear off.

When Ryan arrived at the hospital he quickly changed into crisp green scrubs and emerged from the change rooms to see his first patient being wheeled through into the operating theatre. Dylan Payne was a young mine worker and football player who needed a shoulder reconstruction. Ryan enjoyed surgery and hummed softly as he began the ritual of scrubbing up. A few minutes later, frothy yellow antiseptic running down his forearms, he reversed into the efficient bustle of people preparing for the operation.

He looked around at the team: the anaesthetist—Jim Fletcher, one of the GPs he'd met briefly the previous day; an anaesthetic technician who doubled as a general helper; a scrub nurse who introduced herself as Kelley; and a junior nurse named Janine. They all greeted him civilly and he suddenly felt bad about not being punctual.

'Sorry I'm late,' he said. But he wasn't about to explain that his lateness was due to lingering too long over a huge plate of perfectly scrambled eggs with all the trimmings while in the dizzying company of Tara Fielding.

He could tell they were curious, though, and hoped it was to do with how he performed in the operating theatre—not where he'd spent the night and the early hours of the morning.

But he was wrong.

He should have known news spread like wildfire in a town like Keysdale, where the community thrived on knowing everybody else's business.

Once Dylan was asleep and Ryan had started

prepping the young man's skin Kelley began the inquisition. At least that was what it felt like.

'The last patient is Dr Fielding's father?'

It was a rhetorical question but was a way of letting him know the news was out.

'That's right,' he said as brightly as he could. 'I'll be internally fixing his scaphoid as well as cleaning up his leg wound and applying a cast with a window over the wound.'

'Mmm…we heard it wasn't the only emergency you were called out to last night.' The middle-aged nurse's eyebrows elevated and her eyes twinkled.

Ryan was less than impressed by the familiarity the woman assumed. He had no doubt she was referring to his overnight stay with Tara and his subsequent involvement in the milking, but he wasn't the sort of person to discuss his personal life with a complete stranger.

'Scalpel,' he said sharply, and was promptly handed the instrument he'd requested as well as sponge-holding forceps loaded with gauze.

'How did Tara and her mother cope?'

'Pardon?'

Was she talking in generalities or specifics? He decided to answer as vaguely as he could and suddenly yearned for the session to be over.

'As well as can be expected. I gather the loss of a skilled pair of hands on a family-run farm like the Fielding's can be pretty tough.' He looked across at the nurse and smiled, hoping she registered his expression despite his mask, then continued concentrating on exposing the damaged ligaments and tendons in his young patient's shoulder. 'But I imagine in such a close knit community as Keysdale you'll pull together and help.

Ryan didn't wait for Kelley's reaction. He glanced at the anaesthetist.

'Everything going okay your end?'

'Perfect. Stable obs. What you'd expect with a healthy twenty-year-old.'

'Good.'

Kelley left Ryan alone after that, and despite her inquisitiveness turned out to be a very capable assistant.

Though the morning seemed unusually long, the first two cases on Ryan's theatre list went predictably well. After Dylan an elderly lady was scheduled, with severe deformity and increasing pain from bunions. Ryan removed a piece of bone from her right foot and fixed the straightened bones with a K wire. The relatively simple procedure would make life easier for eighty-seven-year-old Elsie

Tanner, who had worked hard in her family's market garden for most of her life.

His third and final patient for the morning was, of course, Graham Fielding.

Ryan had called in to see him briefly before beginning his list and his attitude, though still complaining, was significantly subdued compared to the previous night.

'I only agreed to this because of Tara,' he'd said gruffly without a scrap of gratitude. 'And because I haven't got time to mess around with referrals to the city.' He'd then lowered his voice and conceded, 'And Tara said you were a dab hand with the knife.'

Ryan had laughed inwardly. He appreciated Tara's confidence in his ability, despite the fact she'd never seen him operate as a fully qualified orthopaedic surgeon.

Pity.

As a student she'd always been interested in the procedural side of medicine. It was one of the reasons she'd chosen the rural stream of general practice training—so she would have the skills to do an emergency anaesthetic or remove an inflamed appendix. They'd talked about her assisting him with surgery. But their plans had been quashed. The accident had changed everything.

But…

Ryan had the seed of an idea.

Why couldn't Tara assist in the OR now?

Operating often involved standing in one place for the duration of the surgery.

Surely a chair or stool could be modified for a surgical assistant who didn't have the use of her legs? After all, she had full use of her hands, and her wheelchair gave her a degree of mobility that amazed him. It could be a way to show her he still cared about her and admired and valued her skills as a doctor. There was also the element of surprise. It was unlikely she'd even think of the possibility of having a useful role in the operating theatre.

But enough of daydreaming. He had work to do and would have to file away his germ of an idea until another time.

Graham's surgery went as well as could be expected. The fracture in his scaphoid—a small bone in the hand notorious for causing long-term problems if a fracture was missed or not treated appropriately—was fixed with a small screw. After his leg wound was thoroughly cleaned, it was dressed, then a plaster cast was applied from his foot to mid-thigh with a window over the wound to allow inspection and dressing. He'd need a more permanent fibreglass walking cast once the swelling settled. Treatment of Graham's bones had been relatively simple, but the size of the defect in the skin on his shin would almost certainly need a skin graft. That would mean referral to see a plastic surgeon in Bayfield or the city, and Ryan wasn't looking forward to breaking the news to Tara's father.

The operating session finally finished at half past one, and he was due to call in to the garage and collect his car any time after midday. Despite the inconvenience, the competence and efficiency of the mechanic had impressed him. After stripping off his gloves and gown he headed towards the change rooms.

He yawned, suddenly overcome with the kind of satisfying tiredness that came after a job well done. As he changed into civvies his mobile phone rang, and he sighed as he recognised the number.

'Hello, Shannay. What's up?'

Whenever his ex-wife rang him while he was working he had a sense of doom. She was usually embroiled in some self-centred mini-crisis that involved off-loading their daughter at short notice. Of course he didn't mind. He loved Bethany and treasured any extra time he had with her. But sometimes it just wasn't convenient—like now. He reminded himself he shouldn't jump to conclusions.

'Nothing serious,' she said breathlessly, as if she was in a hurry. 'I just need to talk. Is it convenient?'

'I guess so.' He began walking down the corridor towards the hospital exit.

'Right. Well, I have some really good news.' She paused, as if waiting for a response, but Ryan waited for her to continue. 'Some fabulous news.'

He reached the vehicle and opened the door, settling into the driver's seat to hear Shannay's *fabulous news.*

'Yes?' he finally said, in an endeavour to hurry her up. His stomach gave an impatient growl.

'I went for an interview last month and didn't think I had a chance but they contacted me this morning. I rang you twice but the dragon who had your mobile said you were operating and you could only be disturbed if it was a life-or-death emergency.' She giggled and Ryan realised Shannay was still just as immature as when they'd divorced. 'I thought of making something up.'

'Who? Who contacted you?'

She'd successfully aroused his curiosity, but he wondered why it was so important to inform him.

'The airline. Trans Jet. I'm sure I told you. I really want to become a flight attendant, you know, before I get too old.

That was news to him. His heart dropped but he had to ask.

'What about Bethany?'

'Well, that's the thing. I have to move to Sydney for training. My hours are going to be all over the place and I start next weekend. Ah…you'll have to take her. That's why I wanted to let you know as soon as I found out—so you'd have time to make arrangements.'

'A week!' He couldn't keep the frustration from his voice.

'The training's only for three months. A trial period. And if everything goes okay I might get to be posted back here.'

'Look, I'll be back tonight and I'll come round to see you tomorrow.'

The anger welled in his gut but he didn't want to get into an argument. With Shannay it always ended in tears, and there was never any satisfactory resolution. He needed time to think.

He needed time to work out what was best for Bethany.

CHAPTER SIX

RYAN wasn't sure whether to grin or snarl. He'd been to see Shannay and was bitterly disappointed he'd been denied the pleasure of seeing his daughter. Beth was away on a play date with one of her young friends.

But the visit had definitely been worthwhile. Despite what he could only construe as a misguided attempt by Shannay to seduce him, he'd gleaned the information he needed.

Yes, Shannay was packing her bags and moving to Sydney in a week's time.

No, there was definitely no alternative to Ryan taking over his daughter's care.

Yes, of course Shannay would miss the lively four-year-old, but it was *a once in a lifetime opportunity.*

And, yes, Ryan would find some way of caring for his daughter, even if it meant taking time off work.

The icing on the cake was that he'd negotiated to

apply for full custody of Beth, and to his surprise Shannay had offered little resistance. She was focused on the present and her own needs, and was as self-interested as when they'd divorced. Their ten-year age difference seemed more pronounced than it had ever been.

Ryan put on a soothing classical CD and made himself a strong cup of coffee.

He closed his eyes. He'd do it, but he wasn't exactly sure how.

'Can I have a quiet word with you, Tara?' Rob Whelan said in his usual calm but assertive voice.

Tara wasn't the least surprised when her employer requested he talk to her privately. It was Sunday afternoon and she was visiting her father, who was as grumpy as ever after receiving the news that heavy farm work was out of the question for the best part of the next two months. Despite Tara's protests he had apparently told Rob all about her marriage to Ryan and the circumstances surrounding their divorce as an explanation for his dislike for the man who had so skilfully treated his broken bones. Rob had taken on the role of moderator.

'Dr Dennison wanted to see you personally, but he was called away to a family emergency. He asked me to give his apologies and tell you every-thing went very well, but he wants you to see a plastic surgeon.'

Rob had patiently explained the reasons to her father, and handed him a referral letter for a Perth specialist who consulted at Bayfield once a fort-night. Fortunately Graham had a deep respect for the experienced GP. Although Tara's father obvi-ously hadn't liked what he was hearing, he'd man-aged to control his temper and agreed to travel to Bayfield as soon as an appointment could be made.

As Rob left the small private room Tara glanced at her mother, who sat holding Graham's hand. She then shifted her attention to her father.

'Dr Whelan wants to talk to me. I'll be back as soon as I can. Okay, Dad?'

Graham nodded and Tara felt his gaze burning into her back as she left the room. She knew her father would never change, but she also knew that if you tried hard enough to penetrate his crusty shell you might find he actually had a heart—a big heart—that was capable of breaking. She didn't want that to happen again, but she had the feeling if the Fielding family's dirty washing was aired publicly it would result in considerable pain—and not only for her father.

Rob waited outside the door and directed Tara to the small meeting room at the end of the ward. She wheeled her way along the corridor and into the room. Her companion followed, closed the door and sat down opposite her. He took a deep, sighing breath.

'I suppose you have an idea of what I want to talk about?'

'Ryan Dennison…and me…'

'That's right.' Rob Whelan paused and rubbed his forehead, but the creases of his frown remained. 'You might think it's none of my business—your personal life before I met you, before I employed you—but I feel if we discuss it now things are less likely to get out of hand.'

'Things? What things?' Tara was aware of an increase in her heart-rate and the overpowering need for fresh air. She began to perspire, and could feel the anxiety building inside like a balloon about to burst at any moment.

Rob picked up on her distress.

'Are you all right, Tara?' He laid his hand on her forearm but it gave little reassurance, and the more she tried to control her panic, the more out of control she felt.

'Er… It just feels stuffy in here. I feel hot. Maybe

I've had too many coffees. And I haven't had much sleep in the last couple of days.' She managed a shaky smile. Her history of panic attacks was something else her boss didn't know about, and she didn't want him to find out now.

Rob left his seat and opened the window. It took a couple of minutes because the catch was jammed. Tara used the precious time to take some slow, deep, relaxing breaths and focus her attention away from her symptoms. Without any conscious effort she began to think of Ryan, and Rob's words rattled through her mind.

How had he explained Ryan's rapid departure after his Saturday morning operating session?

A family emergency?

She'd been preoccupied with her father and his negative attitude to everything and anything but she felt sure that was what Rob had said. Her heart missed a beat as she speculated what it could be. Had something happened to his parents; his ex-wife; his younger sister…or his daughter?

A light breeze brushed her cheeks and the coolness was like an injection of the calm she desperately needed. Suddenly she wanted to know.

Rob came back and sat down, a look of concern on his face.

'Feel better?'

Tara nodded. 'You said Ryan left yesterday because of some emergency? I know I'm probably out of line asking, but—'

'It's okay. Dr Dennison told me he had to go back at short notice to look after his daughter. He didn't give me the impression it was a secret, so I'm sure he wouldn't mind me telling you.'

'His daughter?'

'Yes. You knew he had a child from his second marriage, didn't you?'

Tara cleared her throat.

'Of course. So it wasn't really an emergency?'

He grinned. 'I was the one who called it a family emergency. And what I've told you is all I know. Sorry. But we're getting off track. I wanted to talk to you about how you feel about Dr Dennison working in Keysdale. I gather it's not general knowledge in the town that you were husband and wife and… well…with your father's attitude, I need to make sure what happened in the past isn't going to affect your work in any way.'

'Oh.' She understood where her boss was coming from but wasn't sure how to answer. The presence of Ryan in her life after an absence of almost eight years had certainly scrambled her emotions, but she hoped she'd be able to make sense of what was happening and that it wouldn't interfere with her work. Of course it all depended on how quickly the gossip spread through the close-knit town once the connection was made between Ryan and her accident. She was prepared to brace herself for the worst. She still hadn't answered Rob's question.

'I can't think of any reason it should.' A little white lie wouldn't do any harm, she thought as she bravely continued, 'I no longer have strong feelings, either negative or positive, towards Ryan Dennison, so my work wouldn't be affected. After all, we'll probably rarely see each other. I assure you, you have no reason to be concerned.'

'And if history turns into gossip?'

'I think we should deal with that if it happens,' Tara replied, more confidently than she felt.

Rob Whelan smiled and briefly laid his hand on hers.

'Good, that's settled, then. I'll let you go back to see your father.'

Although fitting the early-morning milking into her already full routine was a challenge for Tara, it at least stopped her from thinking about Ryan. In fact she had little time to think about anything other than work on the farm, her time at the clinic and her efforts to placate her father's frustration at being so helpless.

It was a week to the day since Graham's accident and he'd been discharged from hospital the previous morning—on the condition he limited his activities to simply walking with crutches and carrying out the twice daily exercises the physio had recommended. He'd also been provided with a list of things he *wasn't* allowed to do, and Jane had been given the unenviable job of supervising him.

As if she didn't have enough to do.

Of course he grumbled about everything, despite the fact his co-operation would expedite his recovery. Fortunately one bright light shone out of the gloom. The plastic surgeon was happy with the wound on Graham's leg and pronounced that a skin graft wasn't necessary. If kept meticulously clean and free of infection the wound should heal naturally, he'd said.

Tara shifted her thoughts to the working day ahead as her mother followed her out to her car. She'd negotiated with Rob Whelan to start her clinic sessions an hour later and finish later, but even with the extra hour, and the help of the dairyman on the days she worked, she still battled to get ready for work on time.

'Have you got a busy day today?' Tara's mother asked wearily as she moved the wheelchair ready to put in the back of the car.

'Close to fully booked when I last checked before I left on Wednesday.'

Tara sighed.

She loved her work, but the strain of extra duties on the farm, her father's grumpiness, her mother's self-sacrificial patience and the messy business of her past relationship with Ryan Dennison threatening to come out in the open for public dissection added another dimension to her ever-present weariness.

'So you'll probably be home late?'

'I'm sorry, Mum. If there was any way I could take time off, I would. But with Lindley on maternity leave and the new registrar not starting until next month I feel I'd let the team down.'

'I know. I'm not complaining. Dr Whelan and Ryan have shown endless patience with your dad, so I have nothing but praise for them. And I know how important your work is for you.'

Yes, it was. Her mother was right. Not only was her job satisfying but it got her out of the house, away from the farm; it gave her a sense of self-worth in an environment in which she at least had some degree of control.

Tara smiled and nodded agreement.

'I'll see you this evening.' She paused a moment. 'And don't let Dad get you down.'

Her mother frowned. 'He's getting under my feet already and it's only his second day home. But we'll survive. We've coped with a lot worse than this.'

Tara reached out through the window, grasped her mother's hand and gave it a quick squeeze before she drove slowly off, Jane's words echoing in her mind.

We've coped with a lot worse than this.

Did she mean the dreadful experience of Tara's birth, when Jane had nearly lost her precious daughter? Tara's mother had only told the story once—probably because it was so painful for her to remember that with the complicated delivery of her first baby she'd sacrificed the chance to have any more children. Or was she referring to the anguish, pain and grief her parents had endured after her accident? Did she mean the loss of a future, loss of the rose-coloured dream she'd had for her only child? Jane had had more than her fair share of suffering and disappointment.

But there was no point in dwelling on a past she couldn't change. All Tara could do was play the cards she had left in the best possible way.

Tara slid a pop-rock CD from the early noughties into the player and turned the volume up loud, but the music didn't have the effect she wanted. Rather than filling her mind with pleasant thoughts of vicarious love, hope and fantasy, it just brought back memories. Ryan had given the disc to her. She'd lost count of the times she and Ryan had slow-danced to the caressing monotone throb of the female lead singer's voice. The number of times that seductive, rhythmic intimacy had led to…

She jabbed the off button with her index finger and accelerated down the narrow country road in silence. When she arrived at Keysdale Medical Clinic she had her emotions back in order. Grabbing her mobile phone from her pocket she dialled the familiar number.

'Hi, it's Tara,' she said brightly. 'Can you come out and help me with my chair?'

Pippa Morgan.

The teenager's name had been added to the end of Tara's morning consulting list in the space which was reserved for 'book on the day' patients: those who were not seriously ill but who had problems that needed dealing with urgently. Tara wondered if Ryan would be prepared to offer advice if the girl's problem was related to her arthritis. She decided she'd give him a quick call before his morning got too hectic.

She dialled the number of the specialist clinic and waited for several rings before the message on his answer-machine kicked in. Tara recognised the voice of Liz the receptionist stating that the rooms were unattended until one p.m. and to leave a message or ring the hospital number if it was an emergency.

Strange.

The previous week Ryan had started at eight-thirty. But there was most likely a simple explanation. Maybe he'd been called to an emergency; perhaps he'd reorganised his operating times; or he could be sick. There'd been a particularly virulent flu going around Keysdale the past few weeks, and doctors, especially out-of-towners, weren't immune to illness. She glanced at her watch and noticed it was after ten. She was already running late and decided she didn't have time to dwell on why Ryan had taken the morning off. In fact it was none of her business. If it turned out she needed his advice, she'd ring later.

Her morning consulting went smoothly, and she was only running half an hour late when she called her last patient in at one o'clock.

'Pippa, come in.' Tara smiled at the young woman and beckoned her to proceed down the corridor. Although she was walking unaided, Pippa's body tensed every time she put weight on her right leg and her limp was more pronounced than Tara remembered from when she'd seen her patient about a month ago.

When they reached the consulting room Pippa went in and sat down slowly. It looked as if every movement aggravated her pain, but Tara vowed to remain cheerful and positive. There was always a bright side, no matter how bad things seemed to be, she reminded herself. Tara had been in the same place Pippa was in now, and had survived without someone who knew what it was like to show the way.

'Good to see you on your feet.' Tara offered an encouraging smile. 'But it looks like you're struggling. What can I do to help?'

'I've run out of my painkillers. Sorry to bother you with something like this, but I was booked to see the new specialist today and I thought he might prescribe something different.'

'You had an appointment to see Dr Dennison?' Tara's curiosity was aroused.

'That's right. But Liz rang yesterday and said Dr Dennison wasn't coming in this week at all. The earliest she could make another appointment was three weeks away. I couldn't wait until then.'

'No, of course not. I wouldn't expect you to wait a couple of days, let alone weeks. You did the right thing.'

Pippa grimaced as she repositioned herself on the chair.

'Is the pain still mainly in your hips?'

'Yes, though I'm still getting stiffness in my hands. Probably something to do with the cold mornings we've had lately.'

Tara thought of how chilly it had been in the milking shed the last few mornings and gave an involuntary shiver.

'I mentioned last time about warm water, didn't I?'

Pippa laughed. 'Mum won't let me forget it. She reckons you're a genius. Sometimes I wish I hadn't *shared* with her.'

'You mean you have no excuse for not washing the dishes in the morning now?'

'You guessed it.' She paused, and then continued with a serious face. 'Having my hands in warm water for ten minutes or so in the morning really helps.' The smile returned. 'But Mum says the downside is that she's had to postpone getting the dishwasher Dad promised a few months ago.'

Tara admired the teenager's positive attitude and never-ending courage. It was one thing to cope with limited mobility, but to be in near constant pain... Well, Pippa deserved all the help she could get.

'What time of day is the worst for you?'

'Probably the evenings—especially on the days I travel to uni.'

Tara made a minor change to Pippa's prescription for analgesia and printed it out.

'I've increased the quantity you get each month, so you can take an extra one or two tablets of the short-acting painkiller if you need it.'

'Thanks.' Pippa took the prescription, folded it and put it in the pocket of her jeans.

'Is there anything else you need?'

'No, and I really appreciate you seeing me at short notice. Thanks again.' She made a move to get out of her chair and struggled to stand, but once she was on her feet her movement was freer. She walked slowly to the doorway and when she reached the door paused and turned.

'Is Dr Dennison a good surgeon?' she said with a slight smile.

'Excellent. One of the best. If you need an operation you'd be in safe hands.'

'Good.' Pippa's smile turned into a grin. 'I've heard he's drop-dead gorgeous, and single as well.'

Tara smiled. 'Just what the doctor ordered,' she said quietly as Pippa set off slowly down the corridor.

CHAPTER SEVEN

THE previous week had turned out to be a disaster for Ryan. Organising childcare at short notice had not been as easy as he'd hoped. And Shannay was no help at all. Once she'd made the decision to hand over responsibility for Bethany to him, her sole focus of attention had seemed to be on Sydney and her exciting future as a flight attendant. Ryan couldn't help wondering how long her enthusiasm would last—especially when she discovered that, as well as the veneer of glamour and limitless free travel, there was actual work involved. At least their daughter wouldn't be subjected to yet another series of disruptions, though.

Would she?

Not if he could possibly help it.

But as the week drew to a close the odds seemed to be stacked steeply against him.

All he needed was a nanny who was prepared to do the odd hours he was requesting, including around-the-clock care while he was away. He also wanted someone who would be available at short notice when he was summoned to the hospital on the nights and weekends he was on call. The ideal situation would be a live-in nanny who had no weekend or evening commitments and a non-existent social life on the weekends.

But such a person didn't seem to exist.

Was he asking the impossible?

Then a totally unexpected notion popped into his overstressed mind. He tried to dismiss it, but it kept bouncing back.

What he needed was…*a wife*!

A totally preposterous idea. Where on earth had the thought come from?

He'd tried marriage—twice—and had proved he was no good at it. He'd been rejected by his first wife because she couldn't even envisage continuing to live with him after what he'd done. And Shannay… He'd been blinded by her charisma and infatuation and not realised they'd been too different to sustain any kind of long-term relationship.

No, he definitely *didn't* need a wife. He was going to do the best he could and give everything he had to make sure Bethany had stability in her life as well as an abundance of love.

He could do that.

As a *single* dad.

But, despite all the rational reasons he shouldn't, he still burned a candle for Tara, and wondered if she'd been telling the entire truth when she'd revealed she was pleased he had remarried and had a child. She would make a wonderful mother, and it was a tragedy she seemed to be denying herself the experience because of her physical problems. He felt sure there'd be a way to overcome them. He held the old-fashioned belief that loving parents in a stable home was the most important thing in bringing up children.

Would Bethany be a complication in their tentative new friendship? Did he have the courage to ask her how Tara really felt? Was she envious of him?

Maybe he'd never know.

But he wished he had someone to talk to now—to give him advice; to tell him he was doing the right thing; to reassure him there was no need to panic. And he wished that person was Tara. She would know what to do.

He'd reluctantly cancelled his sessions at Keysdale for the week and had spent the morning interviewing the last of the candidates the nanny agency had sent. He'd not been comfortable with any of the five women he'd seen and he was starting to feel desperate. He was picking up Bethany that afternoon and had planned to be back at work on Monday, in fact he had a full theatre list which would be difficult to cancel. Liz had competently taken care of his Keysdale days.

'Don't you worry about a thing at this end,' she'd said with a confidence he'd already come to trust. 'Just do what you have to do.' She'd hesitated. 'And if you need any more time off—'

He'd assured her a week was enough, but now he wasn't so sure.

He was due to pick up Bethany in less than an hour. Fortunately it was his usual access weekend, so he wasn't on call and was looking forward to spending quality time with her. But he still hadn't managed to find someone suitable to pick Bethany up from day care or stay over when he was on call, let alone look after her on the days he went to Keysdale.

A cloud of gloom descended. Perhaps he'd made the wrong decision. Maybe he should have insisted Shannay give him more time. Maybe the prospect of finally acquiring custody of Bethany had clouded his judgement.

He wondered if it was too late to change his mind.

He went to the kitchen to make a cup of coffee.

He needed a boost before he made the short journey to collect his daughter. As he was about to sit down to drink the hot black brew his mobile phone rang.

'Hello—Ryan Dennison,' he said wearily, not recognising the caller's number.

'Dr Dennison.'

He identified the voice immediately and wondered what Liz could want at four o'clock on Friday afternoon. He assumed she was calling from her own personal phone.

'Liz, what can I do for you?'

'It's more what I can do for you.' She chuckled and he let her go on. She'd already aroused his curiosity. 'Do you still need someone to look after your daughter while you're working?'

Something snapped inside and he felt like pouring his heart out to the middle-aged woman he'd met barely a week ago. But he didn't want to burden her with his troubles, so pulled himself together and said calmly, 'I am. Why do you ask?'

'Well, when you told me last week what you were looking for—the unusual hours, being available at short notice—I suspected it was going to be no easy task to find someone.'

'And? Go on.' Ryan found himself steadying his

suddenly erratic breathing and praying for an unlikely miracle.

'I put some feelers out and thought of my cousin,
Christine.'

'Your cousin?'

'She's about my age, widowed, has one grown-up
son away at college and lives locally. In fact she's
living with us at the moment, because she's just
finished a job as a governess on a cattle station in
the Pilbara.'

Liz paused for breath but Ryan wasn't about to
interrupt. So far the woman sounded perfect. He
was waiting for the catch.

'The family's youngest child left for boarding
school at the beginning of term, so Christine found
herself out of a job and without a home. She has excellent references and loves kids. She would have
had a tribe herself if her husband hadn't been killed
in a farm accident.'

'She never remarried?'

'No. She says she's set in her ways now, and as
long as she has a job involving children… But it's
probably best you ask her yourself. That's if you're
interested?'

'Oh, yes, I'm definitely interested.' Ryan tried,
unsuccessfully, to quell the overwhelming relief

in his voice. 'When can I see her? I could drive down to Keysdale tomorrow, or Sunday. Of course I'd have Bethany with me, but that shouldn't be a problem, should it?'

'Hang on—slow down. There's one thing I said I'd mention before you get too excited,'

Ryan's heart dropped. There was always a 'but' and he was about to find out what it was. He suspected the picture Liz had painted of her cousin was too good to believe.

'And what's that?'

'She would prefer a live-in job. Otherwise she'd have to find a place to rent in the city. She basically said she couldn't afford it.'

Ryan's crinkled brow relaxed and he broke into a grin. She sounded better than perfect.

'So when can I meet her?' he repeated. The future had suddenly taken on a rosy glow, and if Liz had been standing in front of him he would have enfolded her in the warmest hug laced with gratitude and hope. It now seemed at least possible to give Bethany the kind of consistent and loving environment she deserved.

'She's already booked on the morning train to Perth. She has some business in the city to attend to and we thought maybe you could see her then. You said you wanted to go back to work next week—'

'Would she be able to pack a bag?'

'But—'

'I trust you, Liz. If you recommend your cousin, I'm sure it will work out.' He rubbed his forehead with his thumb and index finger, not wanting to think of any other possibility. 'And if for some reason it doesn't happen I'll cross that bridge when I come to it. Thank you.'

'My pleasure.'

Ryan could almost feel Liz's warm smile bouncing along the airwaves.

The gates of Shannay's townhouse were closed but the front door was open. Ryan spotted Bethany sitting on the step as he cruised past, looking for a space to park. His daughter was perched on top of a pile of boxes and bags which he assumed contained the material detritus of four years living with Shannay.

He felt an unsettling mixture of excitement and nerves as he parked and climbed out of his car. A whole new episode in his life was about to begin, and he hoped he'd be able to live up to the challenge and deliver the goods he'd promised.

By the time he reached his ex-wife's home Bethany was standing at the gate, presumably having recognised his car.

'Daddy! Daddy!'

His baby's voice was remarkably loud, considering her diminutive stature. The noise was certainly effective in bringing Shannay to the door.

Ryan opened the latch and scooped Bethany up into his arms. She plonked a wet kiss on his cheek and then positioned herself on his hip as he made his way towards the front door and Shannay.

'Mummy said I was going to live with you.'

Ryan's gaze locked for a moment with Shannay's before he looked down at the eager face of his daughter.

'For ever!' Bethany added loudly and triumphantly.

Ryan felt an instant of sadness at the fact his daughter seemed to have no regrets at dismissing the time she'd spent with her mother so casually. *For ever*, she'd declared. He wondered if the reality of leaving her home of over four years would kick in when she realised she wasn't coming back on Sunday afternoon. And Ryan was struck by the realisation that *his* life would never be quite the same.

'Are you okay?' he said to his ex-wife. She was unusually quiet.

She shrugged. 'I'm fine. I just want to get it over with.'

And that was it. He finally had custody of his daughter and it was the beginning of a new stage in his life.

The news had filtered through to Tara that Ryan's absence from Keysdale was tied up with problems he had with his daughter. Apparently the child's mother had handed her back to Ryan and he'd been doing his best to arrange care for her while he worked.

Ryan's child…

Tara imagined a pint-sized version of Ryan, with soft brown curls, sparkling blue eyes and a personality that would melt hearts.

Ryan's child…

If things had been different *she* could have been the mother of Ryan's children.

She wiped away a tear and silently reprimanded herself. She'd decided long ago she wouldn't burden Ryan—or any man, for that matter—with a child she was incapable of looking after, no matter how much she yearned to have a baby of her own.

How could she cope with the full-time demands of a baby, the exuberance of a toddler, the responsibility of a child? You needed to be able to run to a child in danger, to rescue a toddler from the top of a slide, to act quickly with speed and agility. Which she didn't have and never would. Children were unpredictable, and the fabric of Tara's life was woven with routine and knowing exactly what was going to happen next. She wasn't one to take risks, not now.

She turned off her computer screen and began to pack her things away. She'd somehow managed to get through another busy week of extra work on the farm and her father's continuous grumbling. A small step forward was Graham's reluctant agreement to help with the farm accounts. It had amazed both Jane and her that once he'd got the hang of the computer he seemed to enjoy it. At least it gave them a break from his grumpiness.

Tara sighed as she dumped her bag on her lap and headed for the door...just as the phone started to ring.

'Damn,' she muttered. She should have left half an hour ago, but had decided to stay and clear the pile of paperwork she'd been ignoring all week. The thought crossed her mind to let it ring, but she knew she'd feel guilty and worry that she'd missed something important.

Rather than do a U-turn, she reversed back to her desk and picked up the handpiece.

'Hello?'

'Hi, Tara.'

She instantly recognised the voice and her heart-rate involuntarily jumped.

'It's Ryan.'

She cleared her throat. 'Yes, I know.'

'I thought I might have missed you.' He paused only long enough to take a breath. 'My last patient for the day is your friend Pippa Morgan and I wondered if you wanted to sit in on the consultation.'

'I…er…'

'Of course I understand if you haven't got time. I can ring you. And you'll receive a detailed letter.'

He was providing her with an out, as if he'd sensed her unwillingness. He wasn't to know that the reason for her reluctance was not because she'd had a long day and wanted to get home, nor that she had another commitment. It was because she could already feel her legs metaphorically turning to jelly at the thought of seeing him. In fact she'd managed to evade him the previous Friday and thought she'd succeeded in avoiding him again.

And her reluctance for face-to-face contact was all to do with failed marriages, lost opportunities and children.

'I was about to leave, so your timing is perfect. I'll be over in five minutes. And thank you. Pippa is a very special patient of mine.' She somehow managed to keep her voice calm, telling herself that sharing the care of a patient was a normal part of the association between a specialist and the referring GP. And that was how she planned to keep their relationship.

Strictly professional.

Now that their past was common knowledge and she had nothing to hide there was no reason why that should change.

'See you in five,' Ryan said just before he hung up.

Tara propelled her chair along the corridor connecting the GP clinic to the specialist rooms. The doors slid open as she approached and she stopped, mesmerised. She shook her head to make sure she wasn't imagining what she heard. But it was definitely real. Liz's unmistakably mature voice was attempting to harmonise with the remarkably tuneful singing coming from the mouth of a young child. She paused a moment longer to listen to the simple words of an ancient nursery rhyme about stars and diamonds, night skies and the curiosity of children. The scene touched a raw spot in her heart.

The song ceased abruptly as she began to move again. The child must have heard the almost silent whirr of her chair's motor.

'What's that?' the little girl asked loudly as Tara approached cautiously.

Unpredictable small children and electric wheel-chairs weren't an ideal combination, but she needn't have worried. A delightfully pretty little girl with straight black hair, cupid lips and huge brown eyes peered around the side of the reception desk. Was it Ryan's child? She looked nothing like him. Maybe she was one of Liz's grandchildren.

Tara smiled. How could she not when the girl beamed, her animated face crinkling in what could only be described as mischievous curiosity.

'Hello, and what's your name?' Tara's tentative enquiry brought the child out from behind the desk, but just enough for her to get a better view of the strange lady in a motorised chair.

'Um…Beffny…and I'm…' she took another curi-ous step forward '…and I'm waiting for my daddy to finish work. Um…he's a very important doctor, who fixes up bones and stuff like that. When they're broken.'

Tara glanced at Liz, who hadn't said a word during the mostly one-sided conversation.

'Ryan's daughter?'

Liz grinned like a proud grandma. The diminutive four-year-old, although she looked nothing like her father, had obviously inherited his charm.

'Yes. Her name's Bethany. Isn't she an angel?'

'Definitely cute, but—'

Tara was about to say they'd only just met and she would reserve judgement until she got to know the girl better. A barrier had gone up because she didn't want to get too charmed by Ryan's little girl. Not yet. It was just as well she was interrupted as the words on the tip of her tongue suddenly seemed pompous and totally inappropriate.

'Can I have a ride on your chair thingy?'

'Maybe later, darling.' The timely rescue by Liz certainly didn't come too soon. 'This lady is a doctor too, and she has *very important work* to do with your daddy.'

The child seemed to accept the explanation and turned to face Liz, whom she'd obviously had no trouble bonding with. Tara felt an unexpected jolt of jealousy.

Jealousy? Why on earth should she be envious of the freely given affection dealt out to the middle-aged receptionist by a child she'd only just met?

She promptly rejected the notion that because Bethany was her ex-husband's child she represented the children Tara could never have. She wasn't the kind of person who would bear a grudge. Not after all the years of trying to cast from her mind any thoughts of the future with Ryan that was lost for ever.

'You can go straight in, Tara. Dr Dennison is expecting you,' Liz said after a brief phone conversation with her boss.

Tara knocked softly, then opened the door as Ryan spun around in his chair.

'Thank you for coming.' He indicated the space between Pippa and her mother with a casual sweep of his hand. 'I've just been talking to Pippa and Mrs Morgan about Pippa's arthritis and there are a couple of questions I'd like to ask you. I understand you've been Pippa's GP for a number of years now?'

'Yes, of course.' Tara looked across at her patient and gave her what she hoped was an encouraging smile. 'Pippa transferred from Dr Fletcher the year I started with the practice.' She stopped to think a moment. 'Nearly five years ago. Pippa was in Year Eight.'

Over the next forty minutes Ryan proceeded to take a detailed history, performed a thorough and complete examination, paying particular attention to the teenager's hips, and embarked on a sensitive discussion of her treatment options including surgery.

'I'd like to order an MRI of both hips, as well as blood tests, before we make any definite decisions.'

Pippa grimaced but remained silent while her mother spoke.

'I've heard about MRIs, Doctor, but could you explain what an MRI is?'

'MRI stands for magnetic resonance imaging, and it uses magnets—not X-rays—that produce magnetic fields that bounce off the body and are turned into very accurate images by a computer. I want a detailed picture of Pippa's tendons, ligaments and the membrane lining her hip joints, as well as the bones.'

'Are there any side effects?'

'No—apart from some people getting a rare reaction to the dye that is sometimes injected.'

Ryan rummaged in one of his desk drawers and produced a leaflet.

'This should explain what you have to do to prepare and what to expect when you have the actual test. I've referred you to Bayfield and I understand it can take a few weeks to get an appointment. Which is not as long as if I'd referred you to one of the city hospitals. Any questions?'

Both Pippa and her mother looked satisfied with the explanation.

'And I stay on the same medications?'

Ryan looked across at Tara and smiled. 'Yes, Dr Fielding is doing an excellent job of managing your tablets, so if there are any problems before your next appointment I'd recommend you see Tara.' He directed his gaze back at the patient. 'And I'll see you again in a month.'

Mrs Morgan stood and helped her daughter out of the chair.

'Thank you, Dr Dennison. At last I feel as if we're moving forward,' she said, with gratitude shining in her eyes.

Ryan certainly had a great bedside manner, Tara thought as she watched him escorting the two women out of the consulting room. By the expression on their faces he'd acquired two adoring fans for no other reason than simply being the Ryan Dennison he'd always been. Her mind began to wander as memories of Ryan bounced in and out of her head—as an impetuous and charismatic uni student, as an attentive and exciting lover, as a loyal husband and now as a competent and caring doctor...*and a devoted father.*

'Penny for them?'

Ryan's words broke into her thoughts and startled her.

'I...er...I—'

Fortunately a small dynamo launched into the room like a pyrotechnic rocket. Ryan's attention was diverted to his daughter, who climbed onto his knee and began relating, in considerable detail, the story of her day.

'Hey, young lady, haven't you forgotten your manners?'

Ryan swivelled the child around so she was facing Tara. Bethany, suddenly lost for words, buried her head in his chest, but the little girl's erratic behaviour didn't seem to worry her father.

'Dr Fielding, I'd like to introduce you to my daughter, Bethany,' he said loudly, with a mischievous grin on his face. It did the job of rekindling his daughter's apparent wish to be the centre of attention.

'Hello.'

Tara chuckled.

'We met earlier, and I must say Bethany has a lovely singing voice. I particularly enjoyed her special rendition of "Twinkle, Twinkle Little Star".' She paused. 'Will Bethany be coming with you to Keysdale from now on?' Tara was curious as to his childcare arrangements.

Bethany grinned with pleasure at what she obviously perceived as a compliment about her singing. She climbed off her father's knee and sidled over to Tara, grasping her hand in what could only be interpreted as a childish way of demonstrating her acceptance of Tara.

'No, this weekend is the exception,' Ryan said with eyes slightly narrowed, as if he was defending his actions. 'Bethany usually stays in Perth when I come to Keysdale. Christine—you probably know her; she's Liz's cousin and now Bethany's nanny— has come down this weekend and is staying with Liz. Christine needed to collect some more of her things she wants to take back and at the moment is attending an appointment in town. I didn't see any problem with Bethany staying here for an hour or so. Liz was quite happy to supervise.'

'So I noticed.' She glanced at the child in an effort to include her in the conversation. 'And you

were being very good for Liz and your daddy when
I came.'

In the next minute or two Bethany managed to
climb onto Tara's knees, and she was suffused with
a warm glow of pleasure at the child accepting her
so readily.

Too readily?

'Can I have a ride now?' Bethany's eyes be-
seeched in a way that was impossible to refuse, but
Tara glanced at Ryan before she replied. He nodded.

'Okay, but you've got to hold on tight.'

Tara executed a perfect three-point turn at the
same moment Liz appeared at the doorway. The
older woman's eyes widened as she took in the
scene. A very cosy scene…

'I was just—'

'You don't need to explain. I can see you've made
a new friend and I don't want to interrupt.' Her attention turned to Ryan. 'I've finished for the day and
wondered if you could lock up and set the alarm?
You're welcome over any time after six.' She smiled,
tousled Bethany's hair and then added, looking at
Tara, 'Would you like to join us for dinner?'

'No, I'd better get home. I'm running late already
and Mum and Dad worry.' The response was au-
tomatic.

'It's nothing fancy. Just a casual barbecue out by the pool.' Liz wasn't about to accept her refusal easily. 'We'd love you to come.'

'Yes, love you to come.' Bethany echoed Liz's words, and that beseeching, impossible-to-refuse expression returned to her face. 'Ple-e-e-e-ase,' she added.

Tara laughed. 'Well, I guess if you put it like that…how can I refuse?' She leaned down and gave Bethany a hug and it felt good. In fact Tara hadn't felt so content in a long time. It felt like… She shuddered in disbelief.

It felt like coming home.

CHAPTER EIGHT

'Do you know where Liz lives?' Ryan said tentatively. Liz had already left and Bethany was fidgeting at the door, impatient to get moving.

'Yes. She's been a good friend of Mum's for as long as I can remember. I used to play with her kids. I haven't been there for a while. In fact the pool's a new addition,' she added as she headed for the exit. 'If you're ready to go I could do with a hand with the chair.'

He nodded. 'Of course.' His tone was polite. He didn't want to put her off. It was a breakthrough that she'd accepted Liz's invitation without a protest.

'And I'll need to ring Mum,' she muttered as she cruised through the door.

But then she stopped, reversed and said something to Bethany he didn't hear. A moment later his daughter was comfortably seated on Tara's lap.

'I promised Bethany a ride. Is that okay?'

'Sure, go for it.'

His daughter started giggling as they sped towards the exit.

His heart skipped a beat.

They looked so relaxed together—his daughter and the woman he had never fallen out of love with.

He gathered his bag to follow them, dismissing any thoughts of reconciliation from his mind. Tara had already made it quite clear how she felt about him, but that didn't stop the fantasies slipping into his mind when he least expected them.

Which included thoughts about a future…that included Tara.

He locked the doors of the specialist rooms and set the alarm before hurrying down the corridor. The scene that greeted him when he stepped outside amazed him, to say the least. Tara and Bethany were doing the two-wheeled equivalent of wheelies around the near-empty car park and his gut reaction was to stop them. It was dangerous. Wasn't it?

But Tara's face was lit up with the child-like joy of fun times from the past and Bethany screamed with laughter as they did a one-eighty-degree turn. Tara appeared to know what she was doing and he didn't want to break the moment. It didn't last long, though. Tara noticed him staring and she slowed down, making her way sedately back to the vehicles. She was breathless when she pulled up beside him, and Bethany began to grumble a protest.

'Sorry,' Tara said. All the excitement that had lit her face a few moments ago disappeared. 'I promised Bethany a ride and I just got a bit carried away.'

'Yes, well…' He looked at the recalcitrant pair sternly. 'Don't let it happen again.'

Ryan's mouth twitched with a hint of a smile as Bethany's expression mirrored almost exactly the mix of the contrition and defiance on Tara's face.

'Apology accepted.' He turned towards his car and clicked the remote. 'Let's get you strapped in, Beth.'

The next five minutes were taken up with sorting out Tara's move into her car and loading the chair in the back. He let her drive off first, and as he reversed out of his space his daughter piped up cheerfully from the back, 'What's the matter with that nice lady's—?'

'Her name's Tara, sweetheart,' Ryan said, hoping for an extra moment to compose his answer, cursing himself for not realising how naturally curious and uninhibited small children can be.

'Okay,' she said slowly. Ryan could almost hear the cogs turning in her head. 'What's the matter with Tara's legs? Why can't she walk? Why does she have to ride in that chair all the time?'

He had no idea what was the appropriate thing to say. He'd just have to wing it.

'She had an accident, Beth, and hurt her back and her legs so bad they don't work properly any more.'

'Oh.'

Ryan tried desperately to think of something to change the subject but he was too late.

'You'll be able to fix them, then, 'cause that's what you do.'

Ryan was lost for words.

If only he could.

Seeing Ryan with Bethany, having the young girl offering the kind of simple, unconditional friendship only a small child could give, and the prospect of spending the evening with father and child had Tara's heart fluttering with a combination of anticipation, nerves and a dash of hope thrown in for good measure. The fact that since Ryan had been back she'd realised she still loved him with the same joyful passion she'd had before the accident had been a revelation for her. She was confused. With her heart, she wanted Ryan in every sense of the word. She'd even dreamed of making love with him and it was magic.

But…

Would Ryan ever want *her*?

Aside from all the rational, sane reasons why another relationship with him would be doomed before it started, she was getting signals that her ex-husband wanted at least to be friends and that he wasn't put off by her disabilities. Might he even regard her as attractive? It was a question she hadn't even considered asking herself until now.

Was meeting Bethany what had changed things for her? Seeing Ryan fall so naturally into the role of father had been a revelation for her. His love for his daughter seemed so natural. Fatherhood only served to make him more attractive to her.

She pulled into the driveway leading up to Liz's house, parked the car and suddenly remembered she hadn't rung her parents.

Enough dreaming about things that were about as likely to happen as the sun rising in the west. She removed her phone from her pocket and dialled her parents' number. Her mother answered.

'I won't be home for dinner, Mum. Sorry about the short notice.'

'Oh, that's a pity. I've made the baked chicken breasts you like.'

Tara refused to feel guilty. She was a grown woman and entitled to have a life of her own. Why hadn't she realised before? Why had she led such a cloistered life? Was it to please her parents? Or to protect herself from more hurt? Or maybe the life she now led had simply become a comfortable habit?

But habits could be broken. Old relationships could be given new life—to her surprise her mind was still full of Ryan.

She took a deep breath and suddenly felt a new freedom—a lightening of her heavy heart, a sense of breaking free. And it all had to do with the man who was about to accompany her on the first night out she'd had for months.

She focussed back on the conversation with her mother.

'That's a shame.' Tara hesitated. 'I'm always up for leftovers. You know my appetite. I'll have what's left for lunch.'

The light-hearted approach didn't seem to be working.

'Where are you going?'

'To Liz Tate's place. She and Steve are having a

family barbecue and asked me if I would like to come over. It was a spur-of-the-moment invite and I thought it would be nice. I haven't seen their re-vamped entertaining area…'

How many other thirty-five-year-olds had to ac-count for every move they made to their parents? She suddenly felt claustrophobic and rebellious.

'I might be home late, but I'll be up early enough to help in the dairy.' She knew both her parents wouldn't settle until she was home, tucked up in her own bed. 'Bye, Mum. See you later.' She hung up before her mother could start grilling her. That could wait until the morning.

A few seconds later Ryan pulled up and parked beside her. She opened her door and began to move towards the edge of her seat in preparation for the transfer. Ryan released Bethany from her booster seat and the child stood quietly watching as her fa-ther lowered the chair and wheeled it to the driv-er's side.

Tara managed the transfer easily, and his daugh-ter seemed fascinated by the whole procedure.

'Daddy said your legs don't work because they were hurt. But he can fix them 'cause he's a bone doctor and that's what he does.'

Tara glanced at Ryan. Why on earth would he tell Bethany that? He shrugged and shook his head.

'That's her take on what I said—which wasn't anything about fixing them.' He looked bewildered and embarrassed, but didn't have time to dwell on what Bethany had said and the implications.

The child, now much bolder than earlier, walked over and gently touched her legs.

'Can you swim?'

'Yes, I can swim.' Tara laughed at Bethany's audacity. 'In fact I'm a very good swimmer.'

'Good, because Daddy said I could go for a swim in the pool, but I want you to swim with me.'

What had father and daughter been plotting on the short journey to Liz's? There was no way she was going swimming, and Ryan should have realised that and not got Bethany's hopes up.

'Sorry, darling, but maybe another time. For a start I haven't got my bathers with me—'

'Oh…'

The child looked disappointed, but Tara wasn't going to change her mind. It was easy to distract her, though.

'Let's go inside. It's getting chilly out here.' Ryan came to the rescue.

When they reached the front door and rang

the bell Liz appeared and greeted the threesome warmly. They made their way to the back patio where she introduced Ryan to her husband, Steve, her son, Gus, and Gus's wife, Rachel.

'The splash maniacs in the pool are our two kids, Bonnie and Daisy,' Gus informed them, after shaking hands vigorously with Ryan and kissing Tara lightly on the cheek.

'And you're expecting your third?' Tara glanced at Rachel's noticeable bump, which she estimated to be five to six months along. 'I don't think I've seen you since you fell pregnant.'

'No, I see Dr Fletcher, and he does his antenatal clinic on Mondays. What with two kids, the farm and a *demanding* husband…' she looked over at her husband and winked '…I never seem to have enough time in the day.' She squeezed Tara's hand and added, 'We must get together for a cuppa some time, or maybe a girls' day out at Bayfield.'

'Yes, we must.' But Tara suspected it wouldn't happen any time soon. Rachel led a busy life. Maybe after the baby was born. 'Do you know the sex?' Tara asked. Most couples were more than happy to find out the gender of their unborn baby fairly early in the pregnancy, and by the gleam in Gus's eyes…

'It's a boy,' Gus said.

A cloud of envy hung low over Tara as she observed the happy family. But it didn't last for long. Bethany suddenly overcame her shyness when Christine emerged from the house.

'I want to go swimming.'

Christine smiled and bent down to pick Bethany up.

'You said you'd bring my bathers.'

The child wriggled to get down and stripped off her soft grey and white striped hoodie, fumbled with the fastenings of her lolly-pink denim overalls. Practical but cute—and very *girly*, Tara thought. How wonderful it would be to go shopping with a little girl like Bethany.

'Hang on a minute—you can change in my room,' Christine said.

At that moment Steve appeared with an ice-filled coolbox of drinks and a large tray of meat balanced on his other hand.

'If you don't mind serving yourself with drinks, I'm about to start cooking.'

Liz added, 'It'll probably be at least half an hour until the food's up. Why don't you two go for a swim? The pool's solar-heated. Steve can lend you some board shorts, Ryan, and I have a one-piece suit that would fit you, Tara.'

'No.'

The single word was out of Tara's mouth before she had time to stop it, and six curious eyes were directed her way, waiting for an explanation. She couldn't tell them her gut response to Liz's innocent offer was all to do with Ryan, though. That she'd been imagining what it would be like to renew an intimacy, with all its associated fervour of needs and desires. But she knew lovemaking would never be the same and she wasn't ready to strip off. There was no way she could expose her body and her vulnerabilities to him. *She definitely wasn't ready.* Not yet.

'Um, sorry. I'd much rather be a spectator to-night.'

Liz threw her an understanding glance, but Tara couldn't bring herself to make eye contact with Ryan.

'No problem,' Liz said quietly. She pointed to the other side of the pool, where her daughter-in-law sat, keeping an eagle eye on Daisy and Bonnie. 'I'm sure Rachel could do with some company.'

As Tara made her way around the pool she saw him on the edge of her peripheral vision, and when she turned to look at him Ryan's eyes locked with hers and she knew exactly what he was thinking. It was like the old days.

He wanted her.

She could see the desire fizzing in his eyes and rippling in the muscles of his slick, bare chest.

He wanted her?

If she was right, what the hell was she going to do about it?

When Ryan summoned up the courage to make an appearance in oversized Hawaiian-print board shorts held up by a tenuous waist cord, with a lime-green bathtowel slung over his shoulders, Bethany was waiting at the side of the pool. He took a moment to search for Tara and noticed her heading for Liz's daughter-in-law. God, she was beautiful. He imagined her in a sexy, skimpy swimsuit moulded seductively to her curves.

At that moment she glanced at him and they connected... She blushed, quickly wheeled herself towards her friend and became engrossed in serious conversation.

What was that all about?

There was definitely a spark. Something new.

Something that gave Ryan a morsel of hope he'd not had till now.

But he didn't have time to ruminate.

'Daddy. What's the matter? I want to swim.' Bethany's demand was non-negotiable. 'The water's warm, Daddy. And Christine says I can borrow some of Daisy's floaty things 'cos she can swim already and doesn't need them any more.'

Bethany had obviously had no trouble making friends with the junior members of the Tate family. In fact one of them was doing a fast dog paddle towards them. She climbed onto the step.

'Is that your dad?' The girl wasn't one to mince words.

'Yes,' Bethany said proudly, to Ryan's amusement.

'And is that your mum?'

Ryan's head spun around to look in the same direction as Daisy, but Bethany still had her attention firmly fixed on her new friend.

'My mummy's gone away for a long time to... um...where has she gone, Daddy?'

'To Sydney, darling.' He managed to drag his gaze back to his daughter, but wasn't totally successful in erasing from his mind his imagined vision of Tara's super-fit body in a swimsuit.

'Who's that, then?' Daisy pointed at Tara.

Bethany turned to see the focus of Daisy's attention and her face broke into a broad grin. 'That's daddy's new friend. She's a doctor too.'

'Is she your daddy's girlfriend?'

Ryan was only half listening to the girls' conversation. He felt a tugging on his shorts and looked down at his daughter. She was frowning.

'What, Beth?'

'Is Tara your girlfriend?'

It took him a moment to take in what she'd said.

'No, she's not,' he said, but right at that moment he wished she was.

Daisy climbed out of the pool and came back a few moments later with a pair of blow-up floaties that she plonked in the shallow water next to him, and then swam away to where her young sister had discovered how to blow bubbles under water.

Ryan positioned the inflated devices on Bethany's upper arms.

'You should ask her to be.'

Fortunately he wasn't required to reply as Bethany's attention reverted to the pool.

'Who's coming swimming?' he said with a grin.

Bethany needed no further invitation as she slung her arms around Ryan's neck and they moved smoothly into the water, where they splashed and spluttered and scooted back and forth across the pleasantly warm water.

As Ryan floated in the soothing water he saw Christine slip into the pool and paddle towards him. When she was a couple of metres away she stopped to tread water and nodded towards his wriggling cargo.

'If you want to have a few minutes to swim on your own, I can look after Beth.'

His daughter made the decision for him as she reached her arms out to her nanny and boldly plunged into the water.

'Thanks,' Ryan said, and his gratitude was rewarded with a wink.

'It's not always easy to relax when you have a four-year-old in tow.'

Christine didn't wait for his reply and headed towards the shallow end, where the other girls were playing, leaving Ryan to do laps. And to think…

He glanced in Tara's direction, but she was still engrossed in conversation with Rachel.

The shimmering reflection of the patio lights in the pool danced across her lightly tanned skin and reminded him of an ethereal fairyland. In some ways she had more going for her than many able-bodied women.

Tara was truly beautiful and alarmingly attractive.

She was strong and courageous.

She was intelligent and caring, and often selfless when it came to dealing with those she perceived as being in trouble.

And she would be a wonderful parent, if her dealings with Bethany were anything to go by.

His heart did a clumsy somersault as a startling realisation struck like a king wave in an otherwise calm and predictable sea. He felt totally winded.

Not only did he love her with every fibre of his being but he wanted to spend the rest of his life with her.

He wanted to care for her, to protect her, to be there for her if she needed a shoulder to cry on or to share the beauty of a spring sunrise, the taste of a fresh-picked peach, the gently caressing waves of a balmy ocean on a hot, midsummer afternoon.

He wanted to be an enduring part of her life again.

But he doubted it could ever happen because Tara had made it clear she didn't want *him* in *her* life in any meaningful or long-lasting way. For her, pragmatism appeared more important than love.

Ryan dived to the bottom of the pool and stroked along underwater until he saw three sets of small chubby feet dangling at the side of the pool.

'Daddy, come on—let's play bucking horses.' Ryan's thoughts were interrupted by the impatient demands of his daughter. He grinned and then rolled onto his stomach, letting Bethany tumble into the water, scooping her up again before her face went under. She gasped, and then squealed with laughter as he lifted her so she straddled his shoulders. He began lurching from side to side.

'More, Daddy, more!' she shrieked as he bobbed her in and out of the pool, splashing great gouts of water in all directions.

The game continued for a few minutes more before they were interrupted by the deep, cheerful voice of Steve.

'Food's up in five minutes, everybody!' he yelled.

Ryan looked around for Tara but she was nowhere to be seen. She must have left the pool area when he'd been engrossed in his watery game with Bethany. He recognised the stab of emotion he felt as disappointment, but knowing what it was didn't make it any easier to bear.

'I'm hungry, and Mr Steve says dinner's ready,' his daughter announced, promptly putting an end to Ryan's introspection. He swam to the steps, deposited Bethany on the top one and lurched out of the pool.

Watching Ryan and his daughter frolicking in Liz and Steve's pool had evoked a mixture of joy and envy in Tara. She felt a little on edge, but also revived. Life was definitely worth living when you could spend a pleasant couple of hours in the company of friends who expected nothing more of you than that you have a good time.

Of course she had no idea what Ryan's expectations were. It was probably big-headed of her to think he had any expectations at all. He was friendly enough, but his focus—and rightly so—had been on his daughter, who was an absolute delight. Maybe she'd imagined the sensual connection she'd felt buzz between them earlier.

She suddenly felt the chill of a clear, moonlit night and realised the front of her shirt was soaking, and she had a substantial damp patch on her trousers from bouncing a small but very wet child on her knees a few minutes ago. Rachel had excused herself so she could help her daughters into dry clothes and Tara realised she should change herself.

She wheeled herself into her hostess's kitchen, where Liz and Christine were tossing salads and adding garnish at the last minute.

Liz looked up when she heard the door slide open. She smiled.

'Enjoying yourself?'

'Definitely.' Tara paused, reluctant to interrupt the food preparation, but she was feeling colder and battled to keep her teeth from chattering. 'I wondered if I could borrow a towel—maybe a pullover? I seemed to have got a bit wet.'

Liz left what she was doing and came close enough to do a full inspection. At that moment Tara could no longer stop the shivering.

'Oh, you poor love. You need a dry change of clothes. Come with me.'

'But—' Liz read her mind and glanced at the food.

'That can wait for a few minutes. Your wellbeing is more important.'

Tara followed her down a passageway and was led into the master bedroom. Liz spread an array of clothes across the bed, fetched a fluffy towel and said she would leave Tara to get changed. Liz closed the door, but Tara felt more comfortable sliding the lock on the knob to ensure her privacy.

In the *en-suite* bathroom she peeled off her wet clothes and dried herself as best she could, leaving her still slightly damp trousers on. She glanced in the three-quarter-length mirror and quickly looked away. She usually avoided appraising herself naked. In fact she kept away from mirrors that displayed more than her head and shoulders because she was scared of being reminded of what she had lost. Her pale, thin legs were a symbol of the things she couldn't do any more.

Then she looked back and studied the image she saw—broad, lightly tanned shoulders, well-muscled arms, firm rounded breasts and an acceptably flat stomach. She touched her right breast, tentatively at first, and then with a cautious boldness she hadn't experienced since before the accident. She explored the soft milky skin, the crinkled dark area around the nipple, and then the nipple itself, which was suddenly hard and exquisitely sensitive.

A vivid image of Ryan touching, stroking, exploring and pleasuring her flashed into her mind. Like old times.

There was a soft knock on the door and Tara snatched her hand away, grabbing the towel to cover her nudity. She knew she was fantasising, and logic told her that her dream could never turn into reality.

Ryan had his own life to live.

'Are you okay? Do you need any help?' Liz's quiet voice was reassuring.

'No…' Tara cleared the husky embarrassment from a throat that didn't seem to want to work properly. 'I'll be fine. I'm just getting dressed and I'll be out in five or ten minutes.'

'Great. No need to hurry. Steve's estimate was a tad ambitious when he said five minutes. It'll take at least another ten minutes until we're ready to eat.'

'Thanks, Liz.' Tara's voice was back to normal but her emotions certainly weren't. Her thoughts drifted back to her reflection in the mirror, to the body she'd denied had any worth for so long. To the ugly but also to the beautiful. She wasn't usually a negative person, but since the accident she'd been blinded to the fact she had to accept what she was, the good and the bad, before she could move on. It was as if a part of her that had been locked away for more than eight years had been released.

She was capable of feeling attractive.

She had sexual urges.

She had feelings for her ex-husband.

But could they ever be reciprocated?

What was happening to her? Whatever it was, she knew she had to nip it in the bud before she added another complication to her life—which was overloaded with them already. Her moment of self-discovery was overshadowed by confusion as she slowly and methodically dressed. She combed her hair and then ruffled it into some kind of order with her fingers, rubbed her cheeks to restore some colour to her pallid face and then, taking a deep, calming breath, she wheeled herself through the door and back out to the…unknown.

CHAPTER NINE

RYAN suspected it was more than chance that he and Tara ended up sitting next to each other at dinner. Although he didn't have much time to have any kind of personal interaction with her, he was acutely aware of her presence, her closeness, the hint of chlorine mixed with the fresh smell of a light lavender cologne that drifted into his airspace, the aura of sensuality she didn't even know she had.

'Bethany's a real darling,' Liz said as she passed the potato salad down the table.

It was the kind of statement that didn't need a reply and jolted Ryan back to the reality of the here and now.

'I'd second that,' Tara said with a little shyness in her voice, but Ryan had no time to dwell on her comment.

'She's been no trouble at all,' Christine chimed in. 'Considering what she's…'

It was obvious what the woman was about to say, and Ryan felt embarrassed for her as her cheeks turned a rosy pink. 'She's been used to going to day care and having a nanny, so she takes to new people—especially ones she likes,' he added with a smile, 'really easily.'

He glanced over at the small table where the three little girls were quite happily sitting, eating their way through a plate of chipolata sausages, chunks of marinated chicken and several mini-bowls of salad. Bethany whispered something and the two other girls giggled before the threesome resumed their intimate chat. They were getting on like a rabble of Labradors at their first puppy obedience class—exuberant, curious and totally uninhibited.

'She's made new friends in Bonnie and Daisy too,' Liz said thoughtfully. 'In fact I just had an idea.' She glanced across at Gus and Rachel, who were absorbed in their own conversation. 'Bonnie and Daisy are staying tonight. How about Bethany sleeping over too?'

The offer was unexpected, and something Ryan hadn't even contemplated. When he'd taken on his daughter's full-time care he'd decided to spend every spare minute he could with her. But his daughter had certainly been used to staying at her grandparents' before they'd moved interstate. Beth seemed to be more interested in the company of

Bonnie and Daisy at the moment than she was in his. And if there were any problems he was only a phone call and at the most ten minutes away.

'I'm not sure.'

Liz sent him a look of understanding. 'Maybe we could ask her? You've got an early start tomorrow, and your list probably won't finish until mid-afternoon, so she'll be here for most of the day anyway.'

'All right. I'll ask her after dinner.' It was a shame to interrupt the girls when they seemed to be huddled in a *tête-a-tête* of whispered secrets and shared laughter.

Liz smiled knowingly as the conversation drifted on to the current state of the economy and how it affected the region's primary producers and the very ordinary performance of the local football team the previous weekend. Before long Liz began collecting dishes. Rachel yawned and Steve unsuccessfully tried to refill Tara's glass. Bethany definitely looked droopy, and Ryan suspected her supreme effort to stay awake more than an hour after her usual bedtime was to do with wanting to keep up with her young friends.

'I'd better see what Bethany wants to do before she falls asleep.' Ryan kind of liked the idea of not having to wake a sleepy child and pack her off to Christine before Beth had even had her breakfast.

Bethany must have heard her name, because she stood up, stretched, and then toddled over on slightly wobbly legs to where Ryan sat. He hoisted her onto his knee.

'Have you had a good time tonight?' Ryan knew the answer.

To the adults' amusement she punched the air with a small fist and said sleepily, 'The best.' She yawned. 'Can I come here tomorrow while you're at work?'

Ryan stroked her hair and then kissed her forehead. 'Would you like to stay here tonight and I'll pick you up tomorrow afternoon after I finish work?'

For a moment Bethany's eyes opened wide and she beamed. 'That would be…' Her eyes crinkled in thought. 'That would be awesome, Daddy.'

Christine had obviously tuned in to their conversation and was already bundling the two other girls together, ready to settle them in for the night.

'Let's get you girls off to bed, then.'

Bethany followed Christine without question, and when the woman returned about five minutes later she was smiling.

'Would you believe they were all too tired for a bedtime story? They're sound asleep.'

'Who's for coffee and cake?' Liz asked enthusiastically.

Tara was the first to refuse.

'I really should be going, Liz. I usually don't stay out this late and I've got an early start tomorrow too.'

Ryan checked his watch. Even though it was only just after nine o'clock, he wasn't surprised at Tara's comment. He imagined Graham kept fairly close tabs on his daughter's whereabouts.

'Oh, what a shame.' Liz smiled. 'I'll pack you some to take home.'

'I'll be heading off too,' Ryan said, with the idea of helping Tara. He stretched out his hand to Steve and then gave Liz a brief hug. 'Thanks so much for the meal and the company—and for having Bethany stay the night.'

'Make the most of it while you can.' Ryan thought he saw the hint of a wink before Liz added, 'There's nothing like an uninterrupted night's sleep when you're a parent of a pre-schooler as lively as Bethany.' She paused and then put her arm around Tara. 'And don't leave it so long between visits, young lady.'

Ryan barely heard what she said next as she leaned close to Tara, but the gist of it was something to do with having a social life and cutting the umbilical cord. If he'd heard right he couldn't agree more.

And perhaps he could have a hand in broadening Tara's social horizons.

Maybe he could start tonight.

The realisation suddenly struck Ryan that if he embarked on a physical relationship with Tara it would mean a commitment much more binding than his token attempts in the couple of brief relationships he'd had since his second divorce.

Could he handle that?

It would mean significant changes to his already topsy-turvy world.

It would also mean offering Tara a future she could cope with, both physically and emotionally, and their plans would have to be made together.

How would he handle rejection?

In the best way he could. There were no valid alternatives.

He had to be patient, which was the last thing he felt like being at the moment.

Tonight…?

He'd ask her in for coffee, prepare himself for a

knock-back, and if she accepted? Well, he'd just let the evening happen.

At that moment Christine appeared with two plastic dishes containing what looked like huge slabs of chocolate cake with a big dollop of cream on the side.

Ryan suddenly began to doubt whether he had the courage to ask Tara back to his place.

He rubbed the back of his neck, took a deep breath and reminded himself he had nothing to lose.

Tara was acutely aware of Liz and Steve standing on their front veranda as Ryan lifted her chair into the car. She turned the key in the ignition with a sense of disappointment. It was a little like the old days when she'd been a teenager and single. Before she'd met Ryan. An outing with friends would sometimes end with the feeling that the night wasn't finished. That there was a party somewhere they could go to, or a nightclub that stayed open until the small hours, crammed full of music and dancing and possibilities.

She felt wound up and ready to party. After all it was Friday night and just after nine o'clock— about the time cities woke up. But country towns like Keysdale closed up for the night.

She sighed. She wasn't looking forward to the prospect of recounting every detail of her night out to her parents, but there was absolutely no alternative.

Glancing in her side mirror in preparation for reversing, she saw Ryan heading towards her.

'Don't forget your afters,' he said with a grin, thrusting a container in her part-open window.

She wound down the glass.

'Thanks.'

She expected Ryan to head straight for his car but he lingered, swaying slightly from one foot to the other, as if he had something to say but hadn't decided whether he would or not.

'Is there something else?'

'Ah…yes there is.' He cleared his throat.

Tara's curiosity was definitely aroused.

'It's still early and I wondered if you might like to come back to my place…er…to the motel, for a coffee?'

Tara was totally taken aback by Ryan's bumbling invitation. He was usually so confident and together. She was the one who was prone to bouts of nerves. In fact her heart had begun to thud at the knowledge that Ryan could no longer be *just a colleague.* Whether he knew or not, the fantasies

Tara had had at Liz's, the possibility Ryan could become her *lover*, had put their relationship on a different level.

She ached for his strong arms to enfold her in a tender embrace.

She yearned to feel the passion of his searching lips on hers.

She wanted him in her bed, exploring the new and rediscovering what they'd cherished in the past. Ryan was the only person she wanted to travel the path of her reawakening, and there was an opportunity for their journey together to begin tonight.

'Yes, I'd like that,' Tara finally said.

She let out the sighing breath that had been struggling for release. Ryan glanced back at the house and she followed his gaze to the veranda, where she was just in time to see the front door close.

'I'll meet you at the Riverside, then.'

'Yep, I'll follow you there.'

When they arrived back at the motel, apart from scattered lights and the monotonous drone of television, the place was quiet. Ryan had followed Tara's slow drive to the motel and she'd pulled up next to his unit. Once Tara was settled in her wheelchair he marched ahead to turn the lights on and crank up the heating as there was a definite chill in the air.

'Welcome to the Dennison mansion,' he said with a grin as she wheeled past him into his unit.

She laughed, but Ryan could tell she was on edge. 'It hasn't changed since last time.' Her voice was a little unsteady, and she had a flush of colour in her cheeks despite the coolness of the night 'Except it's a bit messier. Which makes me think this is a spur-of-the-moment invitation,' she added.

'Right. I haven't had time to organise the soft music, candlelight, chilled wine.' It was his attempt to open the door to the possibility of a romantic evening together. He flicked the switch of the main light but left the softer kitchen light and a small table lamp on.

'That's better.' Tara parked next to the sofa. 'Is it okay if I move to the settee?'

'Yes, of course. Do you need any help?'

She visibly relaxed and smiled with a gentle understanding. Ryan felt content that Tara's hackles appeared to be down. She seemed comfortable in his presence, which was a total turnaround since the last time they'd been alone together.

'Do you mind if I watch how you do it?'

She glanced at him enquiringly. He'd expected at

best a reluctant acceptance but she seemed to have acknowledged his ignorance of the practicalities of her disability and was now willing to let him into her world—a world he'd been locked out of for the last eight years. He hoped that at last they were surfing the same wave, aiming for the same place on the shore.

'Why should I mind?'

Tara removed one of the arms of her wheelchair and lifted herself onto the seat with a quiet strength and grace that tripped a switch in Ryan's heart. As she settled—arranging her legs, positioning a cushion at her lower back and moving from side to side until she found the place that was most comfortable—Ryan went over to the small kitchen.

'Coffee and cake?'

'I'd prefer a cup of tea, but a definite yes to Liz's cake.'

'Coming right up.'

Ryan was aware of Tara's gaze following his every move as he boiled the kettle and made the drinks, retrieved milk from the small fridge, rummaged in several cupboards looking for a tray, and finally brought the drinks and set them on the coffee table. He then sliced the rich chocolate cake and served it on two plates with the generous dollop of cream that his kind, multi-talented receptionist had provided.

'Looks delicious—although Liz might well be killing us with kindness. All that sugar and cholesterol... I'll have to work out for twice as long tomorrow.'

'You work out?'

'Every day, if I can.'

Tara forked a piece of cake into her mouth and then licked a trace of cream from her upper lip. Ryan could barely suppress a groan of pleasure, but he managed to keep a straight face as she continued with her explanation.

'I have a small gym of sorts in a room off my bedroom. It used to be a walk-in wardrobe. I do weights. I have a rowing machine, and another piece of motorised equipment a bit like a bike, which helps maintain flexibility and mobility in my legs.'

Wow. No wonder Tara was in such good shape. She'd always been slim, but now she was much fitter. She leaned over to reach for her cup. Ryan's gaze flicked to the smooth, inviting expanse of Tara's neck and the seductive fullness of her perfect breasts.

'You're a very beautiful woman, Tara, and I don't just mean on the outside,' he said quietly, and then paused, gathering his thoughts. There was something he needed to know but he didn't want to upset Tara by asking insensitively. He decided to go ahead anyway. 'I don't understand why you've not married again or at least had a boyfriend? Because you were so adamant you didn't want me after the accident I hoped you'd find someone else.'

She looked at him for a moment, before focusing on the wall opposite.

'I… Because…there was never anyone…er…' Tara cleared her throat, her eyes damp with threatening tears. 'I didn't fall in love again.'

Ryan swallowed some cake that threatened to stick in his throat and then followed it with a mouthful of tea. Tara had not had any serious relationships since they'd parted because *she hadn't fallen in love again*? He felt guilty, and partly responsible for what must have been eight years of loneliness. No wonder her attitude to him when he first arrived had been distant.

But *he* had been Tara's first and only love and she his. He'd already told her he'd never loved Shannay.

'You know that I never stopped loving you and that I still do.' It had to be said—he wanted to make it clear—before friendship turned into something more. He moved a little closer to her and grasped her hand. She mesmerised him with her deep grey-blue eyes. Was it desire he saw in their depths?

Tara leaned across, rested her head on Ryan's shoulder and sighed.

'Oh, Ryan. Why did you have to come back? I had my future mapped out. I thought I was as happy as I could be. And I honestly can't think of love. Not now. It's too hard.'

Ryan gently stroked her silky hair and resisted the temptation to put words into her mouth. *She* had to say it.

He waited.

'There are so many reasons not to even begin a relationship with you. You live and work in the city, you have a daughter. My life…' she paused and a single tear trickled down her cheek '…and my family, my roots, are here.' She moved away so she was staring directly at him. 'There's too much at stake. I'm in a wheelchair, Ryan. I have different needs in a relationship to a normal woman.' A second tear followed the track of the first and she wiped away the moisture with the back of her hand. 'But—'

'Can we try?'

She shivered and then closed her eyes.

'Yes,' she answered in a husky whisper.

Ryan lowered his head and planted the gentlest

of kisses on her cheek, feeling close to tears himself. This was one remarkably brave woman, and she deserved so much more from life than being tied to her parents and the family farm.

'Do you really want to?'

The question was loaded with deep respect and a profound love Ryan had never experienced before—not even with Tara. In a way it was a positive that what might be a new beginning, depending on Tara's answer, would be the gateway to a whole new life; a challenging one, certainly, but one that had the potential to have more fulfilling highs to balance the inevitable lows. He had no idea whether it could work, but the only way to find out was to try.

'I think I do.'

Ryan's heart burned in his chest and a warm glow spread to every tingling part of his body. He'd had no idea he would feel so elated, so blown away with euphoria at the sound of those four simple whispered words. He hugged her close.

'Here? Tonight? Can we start to learn to love each other all over again?'

Tara's reply was husky, but her answer sent his heart racing with anticipation and joy.

'We can only try.'

* * *

Tara knew the emotional stakes were high and she was taking a huge risk, but for once she was making an important decision for herself, and she was determined to follow her heart regardless of the consequences.

'Do you want to finish your dessert? I can make a fresh cup of tea.'

Tara was grateful for Ryan's sensitivity and amazed she felt so comfortable with him, considering they were about to embark on something that could be the basis of a whole new life for Tara.

But definitely first things first.

He was looking at her with tenderness and an empathy she'd never seen from him before. In some ways it was just like old times, but in other ways they had so much to learn about each other. He had the insight to let her call the shots—at least initially. The problem was she didn't know what the shots were. All she knew was that she nursed a white-hot desire, originating somewhere deep in her chest, filling her with a need she'd only dreamed of experiencing over the past eight long years of celibacy. And she'd given herself permission to act on that need.

Oh, how she wanted him.

He ran his fingers softly down her cheek.

'Your skin is so smooth and kissable.'

Before she had a chance to respond Ryan sighed, and kissed the track he'd made with his fingers. His touch was a magical mix of gentleness and wonder. It sent shivers down Tara's spine so acute she felt a trembling in her unfeeling toes.

She opened her mouth as his lips explored, and his tongue probed and searched until he found a spot so arousing she stiffened and a guttural moan escaped from her throat.

'Shall we go to the bedroom?' he said, kissing her again. 'Remember I'm still on L plates.' He sent her a giftwrapped, cheeky smile and raised his eyebrows.

She laughed. The thought of two worldly wise adults in their mid-thirties who had been married before—to each other—starting over like a pair of star-crossed virginal lovers had a levelling but also a very titillating effect. She had no expectations because she didn't have any idea what to expect. All she knew was, whatever happened, she wanted it to happen with Ryan.

'Yes, and it's okay to carry me.'

He simply nodded, before scooping her up in his arms and then tenderly laying her on the bed. He was primed for her already, but he gave no hint of impatience.

Tara lay on her back and reached out to Ryan. 'Come here. I want to undress you,' she said, with a shyness that dissipated as soon as her lover moved close.

Ryan lay on the bed beside her and she rolled onto her side as her deft fingers worked their rekindled magic on the buttons of his shirt. She ran her palms down the bare skin of his chest, savouring the warmth of his body and the wiry texture of his chest hair. He grasped her upper arms in a token gesture to stop her before she unzipped his fly and peeled off first his trousers and then his straining briefs.

He helped her complete the task and smiled cheekily as he said, 'My turn now.'

She rolled onto her back and he began to undo buttons and zips and hooks until he'd exposed her nakedness—and, remarkably, she didn't feel embarrassed at all.

Being with Tara—being *in bed* with Tara—brought Ryan back to a time when making love with her had been the affirmation of a love so strong, so exquisitely all-encompassing, it had never failed to take his breath away. Was tonight going to prove that Tara had the same depth of feeling for him as he had for her? Was it going to mark the beginning of a new commitment to each other?

Perhaps he was expecting too much.

He ran his index finger gently down the sensuous curve of her neck and took a sharp intake of air.

'My God, you are so beautiful, Tara.'

She looked at him and smiled with a warm flush of what he hoped was desire that seemed to wash over her whole body.

'And so sexy—'

She put her finger up to his lips to silence him and then moved her hands slowly, seductively down his chest to his groin, in a way that made him feel he was about to explode with the passion he'd bottled up over all the years of being apart.

He moaned.

'Stop. I want this to last,' he whispered, before nibbling her earlobe. 'I want to savour every moment.' *And to rediscover the glorious past but also to find out how she had changed.*

Ryan explored nearly every inch of Tara's body, and they discovered that in the parts where sensation was unaffected by paralysis her response was heightened. Ryan straddled her hips and blew gently on one of her nipples. It was enough to have her gasping for more.

'Don't stop,' she demanded as her grip tightened on his backside.

So he sucked and nibbled until she cried out in an uninhibited agony of pleasure, and then he continued his journey all the way down to her toes. Although she couldn't feel his caresses she watched, initially with a look of trepidation on her face and then with apparent delight.

Ryan remembered how she'd loved him massaging her calves, finding the pressure points on the soles of her feet and sucking her toes. Although it was different now, those same caresses sent a bolt of need through his whole body and he wanted… he wanted tonight to last for ever.

'Can I roll you over?'

She nodded and grinned. 'It's wonderful, Ryan, beyond my dreams.' She sighed. 'I never thought—'

'I did,' he said softly as he gently helped her move.

When she was lying on her stomach they found pleasure points behind her ears, on the tips of her shoulders, down the length of her spine and, surprisingly, just above the small of her back at approximately the level of her injury.

They made amazing love, with Ryan watching

every moment of her pleasure—and the experience was beyond his dreams. At that moment he knew he would move heaven and earth to win her back.

Tara was incredulous. Although she didn't climax she felt a deep warmth inside when Ryan orgasmed. The most amazing thing, though, was that her disabilities didn't seem to matter any more. She was a desirable and sexy woman. And the person who had brought about the transformation was Ryan…her ex-husband…the man she'd tried so hard to erase from her memory and her heart.

'Shall we finish the cake?' Ryan said dozily as he nuzzled into the crook of her neck. 'I'm hungry.' He chuckled as she raised her eyebrows. 'For food.'

'Okay,' Tara said, and a few moments later they sat propped up in the small double bed, sipping tea and spooning cake into each other's mouths. 'And thanks for tonight.'

'The pleasure was all mine.' Ryan leaned over and licked the crumbs that had settled between Tara's breasts. 'We'll definitely have to make a habit of this.' He grinned. 'Coming back to my place for coffee and cake.'

'I wish it was that easy.' Some of the pleasure and the sense of freedom at being with Ryan evaporated. If she continued to see Ryan her parents were going to be her biggest obstacle. How would she tell them? What would she tell them? She certainly wasn't about to reveal she'd slept with him. But she wanted so much to continue their relationship—at least for the time being.

'What are you thinking?' Ryan said softly.

'I'm wondering what the future holds for us. Revisiting the physical part of our relationship means a great deal to me. Since the accident I've never felt attractive in that way.' She took a deep breath. 'But to be perfectly honest I want more from a relationship than sex, no matter how good it is.'

She blushed. It had obviously taken a good deal of courage to lay her thoughts on the table.

'I want more too, and I'm sure if we both want something enough we can make it work—no matter how many obstacles are thrown at us along the way. Maybe we should just take it slowly until we get our heads around what's happened tonight?' He reached down and found her hand, intertwining his fingers in hers, but their conversation was interrupted by the sound of his phone ringing. A worried expression appeared on his face.

'Hello? Ryan Dennison.'

Tara could only hear it was a woman's voice, and

that Ryan was punctuating an animated monologue with single-word replies. Just before he ended the call he said, 'Thanks for telling me, Liz. I appreciate it.'

'What did Liz want?'

'She rang to let us know that your parents rang her, worried about you and the fact they couldn't raise you on your mobile.'

'Oh, I think the battery's flat.' Tara sighed, her heart suddenly sinking to her boots. She turned on the bedside light and looked at her watch. 'Oh no— it's nearly midnight and I bet they've stayed up for me. I'll have to ring them.'

'What will you tell them?' Ryan said, reaching for her hand.

'I have absolutely no idea, but I don't think they're ready for the truth.'

CHAPTER TEN

TARA couldn't handle trying to explain her way out of spending the evening and half the night with Ryan, so when the phone rang five minutes later he answered it.

'She's just left,' he fibbed, with a calm confidence that Tara could never have managed. She could hear the edginess in Jane's voice, though she could only make out a few of her words.

'I'm sorry I kept her out so late. I understand how worried you must be. But we just got talking and time ran away from us. It's entirely my fault, Mrs Fielding.'

He winked as Tara balanced on the side of the bed to put her shoes on. With Ryan's help Tara had managed to get dressed in double-quick time, and as soon as the phone call ended she'd be in her chair, out the door and on her way.

'*I'm* not sorry.' She mouthed the words and Ryan smiled as, still naked, with his phone pressed to his ear, he walked through to the living room, brought in her wheelchair and positioned it where she could easily slide in to it. He was a fast learner.

A few moments later he finished the call.

'Was Mum okay?' Tara was feeling guilty about giving Ryan the task of bending the truth.

'Anxious, but otherwise quite reasonable. I could hear Graham in the background and I think your mum knew he'd blow his stack if he got near the phone.'

'Thanks.'

She reached out and stroked her fingertips over the smooth curve of Ryan's buttocks and nuzzled a kiss into the wiry fuzz of his pubis. She inhaled the intoxicating scent of soap and their recent love-making. As he began to stir he pulled away.

'Hey,' he said softly. 'Don't get me going again or your parents will be organising a search party. We'll have the local police knocking on the door.'

He pulled on his briefs and slipped sandals onto his feet.

'They'd do that, you know. It's not as outrageous as you think.'

'Which is why we should be getting you on the road.'

Tara wheeled towards the door and let Ryan open it for her. It didn't take long to load the chair, settle in the car and dissolve into Ryan's brief but deeply evocative kiss.

'Now who's delaying my departure?' she said with a wink.

Ryan moved away from the car and sighed.

'Go,' he said. 'Or I won't be accountable for my actions.'

She laughed, wound up her window and reluctantly pulled away, thinking how wonderful it would be to spend the night with Ryan, wake up to the comfort of his warm body pressed against hers, to be his lover. To be his wife?

As she turned into Hill Park Road she wondered if there was any point in dreaming. She was battling to make sense of what tomorrow would bring, let alone speculating about the rest of her life. Her lovemaking with Ryan had been a life-changing event for her. Did Ryan mean it when he said he wanted more from a relationship than simply sex? What she really wanted was the full romantic, happily-ever-after fantasy of marriage to Ryan. She wondered if the reason she'd never contemplated it with anyone else was because she had the same feelings for her ex-husband as before the accident. Had she nursed that frustration for all these years without realising?

And there were so many things standing in the way. It would mean a huge change for both of them, mainly because of her situation, and Tara was fearful of any significant alteration to her structured, rigid lifestyle.

But Ryan had said, 'If we both want something enough we can make it work.'

It made sense and it could happen if... Maybe...?

A dozen questions tumbled through her mind as she turned into the road to the farm.

She needed a clear head to think about the options, and right now she had her parents to deal with.

Both Jane and Graham were waiting on the veranda when Tara pulled up in front of the homestead. Lights blazed from just about every room in the house, and the yard spotlight illuminated the driveway and its surrounds for about a hundred metres.

She knew the atmosphere at the Fielding farm would be tense and she wasn't looking forward to the inevitable confrontation. At any other time the lights would be welcoming, but under the present circumstances Tara had a sudden understanding of the blinding numbness kangaroos felt when they froze in headlight beams.

A moment after she stopped the vehicle Jane was at the window, with Graham hobbling not far behind. Her mother opened the door and leaned close, whispering so that her husband wouldn't be able to hear.

'I wasn't worried, love—well, only a little—but your father started getting a bee in his bonnet about ten-thirty. I told him you'd ring if there was any problem, but when we couldn't get through on your mobile—'

'You imagined the worst. I'm sorry, Mum. I didn't realise the batteries in my phone were flat. I should have let you know what I was doing.'

The choice was between an apology and an argument, and Tara didn't have the energy to protest. Saying sorry to Jane was unlikely to placate her father, though. He was leaning on his crutches just behind Jane, the deep furrows in his brow and the tight line of his mouth reflecting his mood. He was not a happy man.

'Where the hell have you been…?' He paused to squint at his watch. 'Until half past midnight?'

'Shush, Graham. Let's get inside out of the cold. I'll make us all a cup of hot chocolate.' Jane hesitated. 'Or maybe it would be better to wait until the morning to…er…talk.'

Tara had a sinking feeling in the pit of her stomach. She wasn't quite drowning but it was no easy task to come up for air.

'Mum, Dad.' Tara's gaze shifted to her father. 'I appreciate you staying up for me. If there was any way I could get into the house without your help… Um…I'm tired and we all have to be up before dawn so I'd really like to go straight to bed.'

'Yes, love. That would be best. I'll get your chair.'

Graham remained silent, but it wasn't difficult to guess how discontented he was. He turned and headed towards the house, and as he reached the steps of the veranda she heard him mutter, 'I'm not going to let Ryan Dennison take her away from us again.'

Ryan had a full operating list on Saturday, and with the addition of two emergencies and a ward round of his patients in the hospital he probably wouldn't finish his working day until well into the afternoon. With his late night in the company of Tara—gorgeous, seductive, wonderfully sexy Tara—and his full-on day he felt exhausted. The prospect of the long drive back to the city with his lively young daughter minus her nanny had become less attractive as the day wore on.

During a short mid-afternoon break he made a decision. First he rang the motel to check his room was available that night, which it was, then he rang Liz Tate's place. He spoke to Christine and apologised for being late. Ryan had agreed he would take over the care of Bethany when he finished work on Saturday.

'I plan on staying over and driving back tomorrow. Does that suit you?' he asked Christine.

'Thanks, but I think I'll stick with the arrangement of going back on the first train Monday morning.'

'Good, that suits me. You'll be back in time to pick Beth up from day care?'

'Of course,' she assured him, and he wondered what he would do without her.

The practicalities sorted, his mind began working overtime. He desperately wanted to see Tara before he left, and toyed with the idea of asking her to go on a picnic with him and his daughter. Tara and Bethany had seemed to get on well the previous evening, and Beth would act as a buffer between them. Not that *he* needed one, but he thought it might be reassuring for Tara's parents that they wouldn't be on their own.

At that moment the scout nurse appeared in the doorway of the surgery staffroom.

'Your next patient's ready to go, Dr Dennison.'

Right—two more patients, a quick ward round and he'd be finished for the day.

'I'm on my way.'

He'd ring Tara before he picked up Bethany. That would hopefully give them time to talk without the distraction of his garrulous daughter.

Ryan crossed his fingers as he strode back to the operating room. He desperately wanted Tara to agree to his plan.

When he'd finished his hospital duties and dialled Tara's mobile phone number he felt fluttering in his stomach and had to concentrate on stilling the tremor threatening his hands.

Tara's phone rang a dozen times and then went to voicemail.

'Damn,' he muttered, ending the call without leaving a message. He needed a moment to compose one, which was more difficult than he thought.

Last night was wonderful and I'm suffering every moment I can't be with you.

The truth—but way too corny. He knew Tara's mind and it would put her off for sure.

Ring me. I need to talk to you.

Too abrupt. After she got over being annoyed she would most likely worry.

I'm staying over tonight and wondered if you could join Bethany and me for a picnic brunch. Ring me when you can.

That was more like it. Letting her know his plans without being too wordy. She'd have time to think about whether she wanted to accept his invitation before she answered. And if she didn't phone that afternoon? He'd be devastated.

He was about to press redial when the phone began ringing. It was Tara's number. He knew it even without the prompt from the small screen. He cleared his throat.

'Hello…Tara.'

'I'm returning your call. Sorry I couldn't answer. I was just winding up the dairy tour. We've had a busload of Japanese tourists. With Dad out of action, Mum and Pete—from the neighbouring farm—have been doing the milking and I'm the tour guide. I think you know what I mean when I say Dad's not great with his people skills.'

She paused, but began again before he could get a word in. Was she nervous?

'What did you want? I can't speak for long. I have

to go back to the homestead and help Mum with the Devonshire teas.'

'Oh.' He'd finished his work for the day but she was obviously still going full-pelt through hers, and he suspected she'd probably started before dawn. With her late night she must be totally exhausted, he thought. 'I can ring back later.'

'No, back at the house Dad seems to be watching my every move. Best if we talk now. At least I've got a bit of privacy.'

Ryan heard the rumble of a vehicle and the gentle lowing of contented cows.

'How will you get back?'

He could *feel* Tara's all-knowing smile and imagined what she was thinking—that he didn't have a clue—well, maybe not much more than a smidgeon of a clue—about the practicalities of her life.

'I'm on the quad bike. Mum helped me and is on her way back to the house. It was weird, though. The visitors seemed to be more interested in me and my disabilities than the milking. I could tell they wanted to take photos but were too polite to ask. So when I gave them permission they went wild with their cameras. I felt a bit like I was on a celebrity photoshoot.'

Ryan was smiling now. Her enthusiasm for the farm and letting others share it was palpable.

'Sorry, what did you want? I'm talking too much.'

Which didn't worry Ryan. He could listen to her all day.

'I'm staying over in Keysdale. I didn't fancy the long drive this afternoon and I wondered if you would like to come with me and Bethany on an early picnic tomorrow? I thought about ten, and I'd have you home before the afternoon milking.'

There were only a couple of moments of silence before she replied, but it seemed like an age to Ryan.

'Um…'

'I understand if you have to check with your parents.' Silence again. 'And that it's short notice, but—'

'Yes, I'll come.' There was a note of defiance in her voice. 'I'd love to. Will you come and pick me up or would you like me to come to the motel?'

Ryan had been expecting her to *um* and *ah* and was surprised by the confidence of her reply. It was as if he'd handed her a pair of scissors to finally sever the apron strings. Even if she hadn't completed the cut yet, she was at least on the way.

'Whichever you'd prefer.'

'Maybe I'll go to your place. I doubt Dad would give you much of a welcome, and it would be easier for me if we took my car. Would that be okay? I'm pretty sure we haven't any tourist bookings tomorrow. I can bring scones. What time did you say?'

It was like conversing with a tornado. He had to catch his breath, and he wasn't the one talking at a hundred miles an hour.

'About ten?'

'Fine. I have to go now. Mum will be wondering where I've got to.'

'I'll see you tomorrow, then.'

'Looking forward to it,' Tara said breathlessly, and then hung up.

With a contented sigh, Ryan put his phone back in its cover. He felt as excited as a five-year-old going to a birthday party, and he imagined his daughter would feel just the same when he told her.

It hadn't been as difficult as Tara thought. Her father had been busy with the accounts in the small office at one end of the back veranda when she'd broached the subject of the picnic with Jane. After her mother's initial surprise she'd actually sounded pleased about the planned outing the following day.

'Don't worry about your father's reaction. I'll deal

with him. You just go out and enjoy yourself,' she'd said with a gleam in her eyes. 'It's about time you started having a life away from the farm and your work. And I like Ryan. I always have. The truth is I was sorry when you divorced.' She'd paused, reached for Tara's hand and gave it a gentle squeeze. 'You seemed so much in love.'

Tara realised she'd never really talked to her parents about the important things in her life. Of course she knew what a powerful influence her father's strong will had on his wife, but her mother's open support of her seeing Ryan came as a surprise to Tara.

'We were.'

'And still are?'

Tara blushed. She couldn't lie to her mother.

'I thought as much.'

Jane had then gone on to explain her worries about what would happen to Tara when she and Graham became too old to look after her. She revealed that Graham's injury had precipitated talk of them retiring and moving away from the farm. It was one of the uncertainties about their future Tara hadn't even considered.

'I hoped you would marry again—to someone like Ryan!' She'd paused, giving Tara a chance to let the revelation sink in. It was powerful stuff. 'But any men who showed an interest you, you pushed away or your father frightened off.'

The conversation had finished when Graham limped in, asking for a cup of tea, but Jane had said more than enough.

Marry again...to someone like Ryan.

They'd talked of retiring, of selling the farm.

The whole Fielding family dynamic was on the verge of changing.

These were the thoughts scuttling through her mind as she drove along the highway towards Keysdale. Yes, she loved Ryan. In one night he'd released her from the prison of her body and proved she could be attractive, sexy, desirable—things she'd believed she'd lost when her back had been broken and her spinal cord irreparably damaged.

And how did she feel about spending time with Ryan's daughter? Nervous? Uncertain of Ryan's expectations of her? She knew, from the brief contact she'd had with Bethany, that the child seemed to like her and was easy to get on with—not prone to tantrums or overly protective of her father. Her concerns were more about Ryan, and she had a niggling feeling the picnic might be some sort of test to see how she coped in a family scenario. Maybe she was reading too much into the situation and she should feel honoured that he wanted her to spend time with and get to know Bethany better. Yes, she *did* feel honoured, and was looking forward to the picnic.

As she pulled in to the driveway of the Riverside her reverie was interrupted—by the sight of a beaming four-year-old sitting on the step waiting for her. As soon as she saw the car Bethany leaped to her feet, and probably would have run out to meet her if her father hadn't appeared in the doorway and scooped the little girl up in his arms. Ryan's grin was wider than his daughter's.

Her worries dissipated and she wondered how she could have had doubts about Ryan's motives.

When Tara stopped the car Ryan released the squirming bundle and they both came down the path to meet her, Ryan's long stride keeping pace with Bethany's chubby-legged run.

'She's been ready since eight-thirty and must have asked me how long until you get here about a thousand times.'

'Oh, poor Ryan. And I bet you wanted the extra time in bed.'

He leaned into the window and kissed her softly

on the cheek whispering, 'Only if I can share my bed with you.'

She giggled. He was flirting again and making her feel ten years younger. She glanced down at Bethany, who had begun to express her youthful impatience by pounding the passenger door with her small fists. Ryan got the message.

'I know,' he said with a laugh. 'In my dreams—for today at least.'

'Mmm… Pity.' Tara decided it was time to change the subject. 'Are you ready to go? If you are it will save getting the chair out and I can drive.'

'Yes, I have a picnic hamper, disguised as a cardboard box, and a small coolbag I borrowed from the hospital. I won't be a minute. Oh, and I'll need to strap Beth's booster seat in.'

Ten minutes later the food was packed in the luggage space next to Tara's wheelchair, Bethany was safely strapped in the back seat, and Ryan, in the front seat, was unfolding a map.

'I'm not sure where to go. There are a couple of places on the river that aren't too far away and have wheelchair-friendly walk trails.'

Tara glanced at the map and pointed to a spot about twenty kilometres south, where the river seemed to splay out into a small lake.

'Rainbow Pool,' she said without hesitation. 'It's a beautiful place—plenty of room for Bethany to run around in, an adventure trail and sheltered picnic tables.'

'Sounds ideal. Let's go.'

They turned off the highway onto a narrow sealed road that wended its way into the forest. The sun shone brightly but the tall jarrah and marri trees cast mid-morning shadows across the road. Just before they reached the picnic area the trees thinned, then opened out onto a grassed clearing running alongside the sparkling waters of a small lake that seemed to be fed by a tumble of water at the far side.

The ground was firm, flat and easy for Tara to negotiate. She'd brought her manual chair, which was more robust than the electric one; comparing the two was a bit like the difference between a mountain bike and a slick city touring cycle. Ryan unloaded the car. He carried the box and gave the coolbag and scones to Tara while Bethany skipped along beside them both, humming the theme tune of a pre-school TV show.

Tara felt happier and more relaxed than…well,

she couldn't think of a time she'd been more content with life since the accident. She sighed.

'Hungry?'

She was about to say yes, she was starving, because she'd been working in the milking shed and hadn't had any breakfast, but Bethany got in first.

'I'm as hungry as a...um...hippa-pot-mus.'

'Wow, and I thought I was really hungry.' Tara chuckled. The little girl brimmed over with excitement.

'Sun or shade?' Ryan asked when they'd travelled the short distance to the picnic area.

'Has Bethany got a hat?'

There was no need to answer as Bethany pulled a floppy denim hat edged with tiny embroidered yellow flowers from her matching backpack. She placed it on her head and pleaded, 'Can we *please* sit in the sun, Daddy?'

He glanced over at Tara, who was already wearing a hat. 'And I managed to keep her still enough this morning to slather on some sunscreen. Do you mind sitting in the open?'

She shivered. There were still remnants of the early-morning chill in the air and the sunshine would be welcome.

'Yep, definitely.'

Ryan wore knee-length canvas shorts and a black tee shirt with a Bali logo on it. His baseball cap was slightly skewed, which Tara thought was cute. He looked gorgeous in his casual gear. In fact the whole package conveyed the same relaxed contentment *she* was feeling.

The area was deserted—wrong time of year, wrong time of day for crowds—but Tara imagined if more picnickers arrived they might easily assume she, Ryan and Beth were a typical family. In her dreams…

They parked next to a rough-sawn plank table and Ryan began unloading food.

'What's to eat?' Tara asked, curious to know what was in the various bags and packages.

'It's very simple. I called in to the markets yesterday afternoon.' He gave a running commentary as he unpacked each item and held them up for inspection. 'Fresh-baked bread rolls, shaved ham and salami, salad greens, some cheese, sundried tomatoes and for dessert—strawberries and fresh cream. Oh, and your mum's scones.'

By the time he'd finished Tara's mouth was watering and her stomach growled.

'Looks positively delicious.' He'd certainly remembered what she liked.

He handed her and Beth paper plates stacked high with mouthwatering food and then served himself. He settled on the broad timber bench seat with Bethany perched on his knee. They ate until they were full to overflowing, and as soon as they finished Beth was itching to explore.

'Will you come for a walk with me?' The child's question was directed at Tara.

Tara glanced at Ryan. 'Shall we pack up and then go exploring? I could do with the exercise. I didn't have time for my normal gym routine this morning.'

'Why don't you and Bethany set off for a walk? There's a bitumen track just over there. I'll pack up and follow you in five or ten minutes,' Ryan added with enthusiasm.

Could she?

Ryan trusted her with the care of his daughter, even if it was only for ten minutes.

Yes, of course she could. It wasn't as if they were perched on a cliff or next to a raging sea. It was a level sealed path meandering around a mirror-smooth lake.

'Will she be all right?' Tara looked across at Ryan and raised her eyebrows.

'You mean will Beth run into a grove of prickle

bushes or climb a tree and not come down?' He tickled his daughter and she laughed hysterically. When she settled down he sat her on his knees so they were facing each other and said, quietly but firmly, 'You can go for a walk with Tara if you stay close to her all the way and don't go off the track. Do you think you can do that?'

'Yes, Daddy,' she said seriously.

'Tell me what I just asked you to do.'

'Don't go off the path and…um…hold onto Tara.' Looking over at Tara, she began to giggle. 'So she doesn't go in the prickles or climb a tree.'

Ryan seemed satisfied with her answer. She was certainly a bright child and, despite her energy, had been well behaved so far.

'She'll be fine,' he said. 'And if I haven't caught up with you in ten minutes just turn around and come back, and make sure I haven't got stuck in the prickles.'

Bethany was already at Tara's side, waiting for instructions. She reached out to hold Tara's hand—obviously the normal thing she would do when going for a walk with an adult. After Tara had demonstrated that she needed both hands to pro-pel and steer her chair they decided on a compromise, where Beth walked on the path and stayed in Tara's sight.

A few moments later they were on their way— on a journey of discovery.

'What's that?' Bethany said as she stopped to look at a bright yellow fungus clinging tenaciously to a dead tree stump.

'It's called a fungus.'

'Fungus. Ooh, look—there's 'nother one…and 'nother.' She stopped to examine a two-metre-wide spiderweb spanning the pathway just above her head. 'Can't see the 'pider. Might be a redback. Better be careful.'

She turned, waiting for Tara's instructions.

'It's not a redback's web. They live in dark places and have a different sort of web. If you get a stick we can make a way through. A lot of spiders only come out at night.'

'Oh, so he's having a sleep and doesn't mind if we smash up his house?'

Tara was lost for words, not having a clue how to answer the not unreasonable question. She decided to use the 'change the subject' technique.

'Look over there, Bethany. Is that a little beach?'

Up ahead about five or six metres of scrub opened up to expose a sandy beach.

'I'll go and look.' Bethany began to run.

'Not too fast. Wait for me.' Tara picked up speed and reached the beach just as Bethany made another exciting discovery.'

'Come and have a look. There's tiny, tiny little fishies in the water.'

In the blink of an eye the little girl had slipped off her sandals and was wading in the shallows, ankle-deep in the water.

'No, Beth!'

But she was too late. Bethany leaned over and took a single step—which must have been enough to make the steep bank which was dangerously close to the shore crumble. The child screamed as she floundered in water at least a metre deep.

What Tara did next was a reflex reaction.

She pushed her chair hard into the soft sand and when she reached the water tipped the chair over on its side. The strength of her arms broke the fall and in an instant she was dragging herself into the water.

'I'm coming, Beth.'

She might not be able to walk but she could certainly swim.

She dragged herself into the freezing lake and grabbed the child, who was still splashing and sput-

tering. She clutched Beth to her side and manoeuvred awkwardly onto dry ground. As she took a
moment to catch her breath she felt strong warm
arms encircling both her and Beth, dragging them
further up the beach. Beth gasped and then started
sobbing. Ryan released his grip on Tara and hugged
his shivering daughter to his chest.

'What happened? Are you all right?'

'Sorry. Sorry, Daddy,' Bethany managed between
sobs. 'I—I wanted to see…' she took a deep gasping breath '…the little fishies.'

Tara's heart went out to the terrified child. She
was trying to take the blame. But it was Tara's fault.
Useless, hopelessly inadequate Tara's fault.

The old doubts came flooding back in a torrent.
She could never be an effective parent. Bethany
could have died because of her crippled legs, her
false hopes and impossible dreams. To think she
could live any kind of useful life as a wife and
mother was pure fantasy. Her one blissful night
with Ryan had blinded her to the reality of the rest
of her life. She couldn't burden Ryan with a lifetime
of looking after her. He had Bethany to care for, as
well as a full-time job. It was fanciful to think he
had anything left for her. Nothing had changed. He
needed a wife who was complete.

She started trembling uncontrollably.

'Are you hurt anywhere?'

With his free hand Ryan began feeling for bumps, sprains and broken bones.

'I'm fine,' she said brusquely. 'Just help me into the chair and take me back.' She looked up into his bewildered eyes for a moment. Any longer was too much to bear. 'I'm so sorry... I—'

His finger resting lightly on her lips effectively silenced the flood of words that seemed to have stuck in her throat.

'No one's to blame and there's no harm done. You'll feel much better when you're warm and dry. It's been a shock, but nobody's hurt.'

He lifted her into her chair, placed Bethany on her lap, and then stripped off his tee shirt and wrapped it around them both as best he could. Then, despite Tara's protests, he pushed them all the way back to the car, sat them both in the back seat and drove back to Keysdale with the heater on full. During the trip they were silent. Even Bethany was subdued. And when they arrived at the motel unit Ryan offered only token resistance when Tara told him she wanted to go straight home.

'When can I see you again?' he asked as he

wrapped the fleece jacket he'd just brought out from the motel unit around her still damp shoulders.

She reluctantly accepted his help to lift her out of the back seat and into the driver's before dealing with Beth and removing the booster seat.

Taking comfort in reclaiming some degree of control, Tara turned the key in the ignition. The longer she spent with Ryan, the harder it would be to break away.

'I think…er…I'll let you know.'

Now was not the time to try and explain the raw emotions tumbling through her mind. She needed time to put her thoughts in order, to restore a sense of reality, to formulate how to tell him there was no way a relationship could possibly work without sac-rifice—the sort of painful and life-changing com-promises that would tie Ryan to her in a way she wasn't prepared to accept. She wouldn't survive in a one-sided relationship, and that was what it would be. Ryan would be accepting second best—as a lover, a wife and a mother for his child. Although she'd had to adapt to some degree of dependence on her parents she felt the balance of give and take had evened out over the years. She paid her way; in fact her income had helped save the farm when it was close to bankruptcy, and now her father was out of action she was actually working hands-on.

She had little to give Ryan.

Her love wasn't enough.

Wanting with all her heart and soul to have her own child didn't qualify her to be a parent. She'd proved that this afternoon, when Ryan had entrusted her with the care of his daughter and Bethany had almost drowned. How could a woman who was reliant on a wheelchair for mobility possibly look after a totally dependent baby, an unpredictable toddler, a boisterous child? She'd made the mistake of beginning to believe in her own daydreams. With a detached eye she could see how wrong she had been to even fantasise.

And the sex!

Yes, it had been fantastic. But the novelty would wear off. Half her body didn't respond to the physical stimulation they'd both always found so arousing before the accident. Ryan had suffered enough. She didn't want to be responsible for the compromises he would have to make if they tried to heal the deep wounds of their past. She didn't have the energy or emotional fortitude to launch into a high-stakes relationship that had every chance of ending in heartbreak for both of them.

It was better it ended now.

'Goodbye, Ryan,' she said as she reversed away from him, wondering how long it would take this time to glue together the pieces of her shattered heart.

Ryan felt as if all the air had been forced out of him by one massive blow to his chest. Just when he'd thought he was making progress with Tara she'd closed herself off from him, and for no logical reason. Was she so entrenched in the predictable routine of her life that she was running scared? Did the prospect of change frighten her? Was she so tangled up in guilt about Bethany's dunking that she'd lost sight of the fact they'd been making progress in their tentative renewed relationship?

He suspected the incident with Bethany had broken Tara's spirit and eroded her confidence, but he was just as much to blame as her, letting his daughter go off with Tara alone. He should have known Beth often went off track when she got excited. If Tara hadn't been there and acted so swiftly Bethany could have drowned. But when he'd tried to explain the barrier between them had strengthened.

How could he convince her he still loved her and would do anything to win her back?

He owed her big-time, but she had left him with a look that suggested a broken heart all over again. He couldn't live with that, and had to work out a way to get through to her. Maybe he'd start by presenting her with the practical. All the things they could do to make their future viable.

Then a thought suddenly popped into his bewildered mind.

Pippa Morgan.

Tara cared deeply about her patients and especially Pippa. Maybe he could get through to her by means of tapping in to her love of medicine and devotion to her patients.

At the very least it was food for thought, and Ryan vowed he wasn't about to give up the only woman he had ever loved without a fight.

He would use any legitimate means available to win her back.

CHAPTER ELEVEN

RYAN had arranged to meet with Liam Taylor, the rheumatologist who was treating Pippa Morgan. He'd seen the young woman the previous week and her MRI scan had confirmed her right hip was so damaged by the relentless disease she'd suffered from childhood it was only a matter of time before she would be dependent on a wheelchair. If that happened it would probably be downhill from there. At nineteen, when she should be at the peak of good health, her bones would begin to crumble, her muscles waste and her fighting spirit would have to be super-strong to survive.

Surgery wasn't a cure, but it would definitely improve Pippa's quality of life. Ryan wanted to make sure that all the other options had been tried. A hip replacement was a major operation, not without possible complications, and he predicted Pippa's recovery would be slower than normal because of the disease affecting other joints.

Ryan sat in his consulting room at the end of his

morning session at St Joseph's and reread the MRI report, intermittently glancing at the images on his computer screen.

The ring of his telephone broke into his reverie. 'Yes?'

'It's Dr Taylor to see you,' the receptionist informed him. 'Shall I tell him to go through?'

'Thanks, Pat, send him down to my room.'

A few moments later Liam Taylor knocked softly on his door before walking into the room. Ryan stood, shook his hand and gestured for him to sit down. Once the pleasantries were done with they got down to business.

'I can offer her pain relief and restoration of at least some of the mobility of her joint with surgery. But it won't be without some trade-offs. I wanted to check with you to make sure there were no other options for the girl.'

Ryan passed the MRI report to the rheumatologist, who studied it carefully and then looked up to meet Ryan's questioning gaze.

'You have copies of the letters I've sent to her treating GP?'

'Yes. You probably know I've started sessional work in Keysdale, and I've had several discussions with Dr Fielding about Pippa.'

Mentioning Tara made his heart lurch. She'd barely spoken to him since the picnic, despite his frequent pleas not to blame herself for Bethany's misadventure. Of course *he'd* been upset as well, but no harm had come of the incident.

She'd closed her ears and her heart to mention of anything other than work, though. It was three weeks now, and he'd almost given up on any plans he'd had to get through to her.

'Then you know she's come to the end of the line with non-surgical treatment?'

'Yes—unless there's something new. I understand she's even had a trial of an experimental drug.'

'Unfortunately I've gone as far as I can with her, and if you think you can help her with surgery, and Pippa agrees, then I'm with you all the way.'

'That's what I wanted to hear,' Ryan said with a tentative smile.

'Of course she'll need detailed anaesthetic assessment. She's been fairly lucky so far in not developing systemic disease.'

'Like fevers, rashes, muscle involvement?'

'Right. Her disease seems to primarily affect her joints, and the most active inflammation and destruction has been in her hips.'

'If she agrees to surgery I'd want to do it here in the city.'

'Yes, of course, and I'd follow her progress.'

'I'd appreciate that.'

'Had you thought of involving her GP in the operation?'

'Pardon?'

'There've been several interesting trials involving young adults who have suffered long-term diseases like rheumatoid. Getting the patient and the family or carers as well as the GP together for regular case conferences and involving them directly in the decision-making improves the outcome of not only surgery. They also apparently respond better to other treatments like medication and physiotherapy. In fact I've tried it on a couple of my more resistant patients and there seems to be some substance in their conclusions.' He cleared his throat. 'Of course my experience is only anecdotal.'

'Sorry, I don't quite understand how the GP fits in with what you've told me.'

'The GP works actively with the surgeon and patient, including being present and ideally assisting in the operation. The couple of calls I've had from Tara Fielding suggest she cares a great deal about her young patient. It's just a way of extending the doctor-patient relationship—hopefully with some added benefits for Pippa.'

'Oh, I see.'

Ryan had shelved the idea of involving Tara in the OR at Keysdale. The way they'd been communicating lately was matter-of-fact, and usually by e-mail or telephone if it involved patients. On a more personal level their exchanges had been almost non-existent. But… It might be a way to get through to Tara—through her work and dedication to her patients.

'I'd be interested to read the studies. Could you give me details of the publications?'

The doctor smiled. 'I can do better than that. I'll send my receptionist down with photocopies this afternoon.'

They wound up the meeting and after Liam Taylor left Ryan was infused with a sense of hope not only related to a positive outcome of Pippa Morgan's surgery but also discovering a viable way to crack the seemingly impenetrable barrier Tara had erected between them.

He tapped his pen restlessly on his desk and then sighed.

He really had nothing to lose.

He was prepared to put everything into winning Tara back.

Tara scrolled down her e-mails. She'd had a busy day, and it was time to go home, but she preferred to tidy up the loose ends of her week before she left. Thankfully the list of e-mails was relatively short and she worked through them easily—until she reached the last but one.

It was from Ryan.

Even though she knew it would be work-related her heart thudded unevenly and her throat was suddenly dry. The mere thought of her ex-husband did strange things to her body she didn't quite understand. Or maybe she *did* understand. She'd tried to ignore all the signs that indicated she wasn't over him. Despite the rational part of her brain reinforcing that a future with Ryan was impossible, her bruised and battered heart didn't seem to get the message.

She took a deep breath and pressed the mouse button to open the e-mail.

It took her barely a minute to read it...twice—though she still didn't quite comprehend what he was asking.

It was about Pippa Morgan.

Right. She got the bit about the results of the MRI. She understood why he'd want to tell her about the urgent need for surgery, that a date had been set for two weeks from Saturday at St Joseph's, and that he'd organised the involvement of Liam Taylor in her post-operative recovery.

It was the last two sentences that threw her totally off balance.

I want to talk to you about the possibility of you coming up and assisting with Pippa Morgan's operation. Can we meet when you've finished consulting and I can explain?

Assisting with Pippa's operation?

How on earth did he expect her to manage that? Even if she agreed to the outlandish request it just wasn't feasible. For a start she doubted her chair would be allowed into the theatre area, let alone into an operating room. There would be too great a risk of contamination, particularly with major surgery involving bone. And if she did get into the theatre to actually *assist* would mean some sort of wheelchair modification to raise her to the level of the operating table.

Tara hadn't been in an operating theatre since her hospital residency.

Regardless of all her other objections, what if she panicked? She'd turn out to be an inconvenient liability rather than a useful addition to the surgical team. In fact she felt anxious just thinking about it.

Had Ryan lost his marbles completely?

After quickly checking the last e-mail she shut down her computer and gathered her things in readiness for going home. What Ryan was suggesting was impractical, physically impossible and totally out of the question. And she didn't need to tell him face to face. She scribbled a note, deciding she'd do the polite though maybe the cowardly thing and leave a message with one of the receptionists to give to Ryan when he left. But as she swivelled her chair the door opened and Ryan stood in the doorway, smiling with a confidence that bordered on smugness. He obviously wasn't counting on a knock-back.

'Hi,' he said as he stepped into Tara's room. 'Did you get my e-mail?'

Tara cleared her throat, but it didn't prevent the roughness in her voice.

'Yes, just a few minutes ago. And the answer is no.' She paused and took a measured breath. 'I don't think you realise how difficult everyday tasks are for me, let alone the long drive to Perth, and getting some stranger to help me get mobile. And I doubt very much I'd be allowed anywhere near the operating theatres in a wheelchair.'

Ryan moved one of the patients' seats so it was directly opposite Tara and sat down. The intensity of his gaze unsettled her, although he was still smiling.

'I've thought of all that.'

'What do you mean?'

'I've done some research and I'm sure it can be done.' Ryan's expression suddenly changed and he looked like an excited schoolboy about to explain his way out of some way-out, non-curricular misdemeanour to an uncompromising teacher. That vulnerability she rarely saw was back, and Tara decided the least she could do was listen. In fact she was a little curious about this *research* he mentioned.

'Go on.'

'Well, the issue of getting up to Perth is easy. I'll take you back with me after my afternoon clinic here on the Friday. If it's more convenient to use your car I'm okay with that. I'd leave my car at Liz's.' He hesitated a moment, as if he needed an extra dose of courage to continue. 'And you can stay overnight at my place.'

'But…' There were a hundred and one reasons why that wasn't a good idea. Being in the same physical space as Ryan spelled danger. And he had the effrontery to grin.

'Christine will be there to look after Beth, and I'm sure she'd be able to help you with anything you can't manage yourself. That's if you're too embarrassed to ask me to help.'

'You mean with things like showering?'

He shrugged.

'Yes, that sort of thing. My shower's a large one and could easily accommodate a shower chair and two people.'

She blushed at the thought of actually sharing a shower with Ryan.

He seemed to tune in to her thoughts.

'I'm not going to come on to you, if that's what you're worried about.' He rubbed his forehead and his face went into neutral, then he grinned again. 'Not unless you want me to.'

'I don't,' she said, a little more abruptly than she'd planned.

'And even if you did I suspect the presence of Bethany and Christine would be a passionkiller.'

He had a point, but she *didn't want to*. Did she? The thought crossed her mind that at some subliminal level maybe she did. And that was what was alarming her. As well as how, so far, Ryan had thought of everything.

'That's all very well, but I can't see any way of the hospital protocol accommodating my presence in the operating theatre.' She glanced down at her legs and succumbed to a rare moment of resentment. 'I haven't got the use of my legs. Remember?'

Tara regretted the sarcasm as soon as the words were out of her mouth. But she'd loved surgery as a student, and it seemed a little cruel that Ryan was dangling an unreachable carrot in front of her. He seemed to be undaunted by her response, though. He reached out to put his hand over hers. It was an incredibly tender gesture and, whatever Ryan's motives, she realised he knew her better than anyone. He really cared.

'No, I haven't forgotten. You know I'll never be able to forget.' He squeezed her hand. 'But I thought this might be a way to show you I can help you move forward.'

He'd touched on the aching, throbbing centre of her life. She was stagnating and had little chance of moving anywhere. The rut she was stuck in was growing deeper as time passed. Her time with Ryan—their lovemaking and the cosy domesticity they'd shared on the picnic—had opened a window to another breathtakingly amazing world that she'd naively thought was within her reach. But she'd been wrong. With Bethany's near-drowning, the window had been slammed shut.

'So tell me how you plan to make this outrageous plan of yours a reality? I know you're capable of multi-tasking, but I think you'd need a magic wand to pull this off.'

'It's not been as difficult as I'd thought. St Joseph's are quite happy to have you working in their theatres as long as first you fill out the paperwork and second you don't compromise any OR procedures and rules which might interfere with patient safety.'

'Okay, the first part is straightforward, but I can't see—'

'Just let me finish before you make any judgements. You can take your wheelchair as far as the change rooms, where one of the nurses can help you get into theatre gear. Then you transfer into one of the hospital chairs. Before you scrub up you'll need to transfer onto a purpose-built adjustable operating stool.'

'An operating stool?' The idea of such a thing sounded fanciful to Tara. 'What on earth is that?'

'Well, it just so happens…' The pause was tantalisingly prolonged.

'Come on, you've got to explain now you've started.' Much to her annoyance, he'd captured her attention.

'There's an anaesthetist on their staff who had major back surgery a few years ago and was left with weakness in both his legs. He was so determined to get back to work after the operation he had a special seat made. I checked it out last week and got the okay for you to use it as long as Peter isn't rostered on.'

'A stool? I'd topple off if I lost my balance—'

'It has a back rest and removable arms. Mobility is controlled by a joystick and an electric motor, similar to your motorised chair.'

'Is it height-adjustable?'

'Yes, with the same kind of joystick.'

'What about a sterile operating field? I'd be scrubbed and gloved.'

'A sterile soft plastic cover is put over the stick.'

Tara was intrigued. Ryan had covered every objection she had. The prospect of getting back into the operating theatre and helping Pippa Morgan excited her and she was tempted. Ryan read her reaction in her eyes.

'I have some journal articles you might like to read that suggest there is benefit to patients with problems like Pippa's if her entire medical team is involved in major therapeutic events like surgery. Recovery is faster and results are better.'

His research and planning baffled her. She didn't know what to say.

'So you'll at least think about it?' His look was pleading, as if her saying yes meant a lot to him. He'd gone to an awful lot of trouble.

'I'll think about it.'

'Good.' Ryan's posture relaxed and he smiled. 'I need to know by the Wednesday before Pippa's op.'

'I'll think about it,' Tara repeated as she gathered up her bag and medical case and put them on her knee, hoping Ryan got the message their conversation was over. He moved out of the way as she propelled forward.

'I'll help you with your chair.'

Ten minutes ago, before their remarkable discussion, Tara probably would have been annoyed at his offer, but her mind-set had subtly changed. Just because Ryan had presented her with the possibility of not only helping her patient, but also the opportunity to do something she'd never dreamed was achievable, it didn't mean she wanted their relationship to go any further than a professional one. But she was definitely tempted by his offer.

'Thanks,' she said, and they walked together along the corridor. 'I appreciate it,' she added quietly, and was relieved Ryan didn't answer.

Before she embarked on the homeward journey Tara took a few minutes to glance at the summaries of the articles Ryan had given her.

Was helping Pippa worth letting Ryan think he could organise her career?

Maybe it was.

It certainly gave Tara something to think about.

CHAPTER TWELVE

IT HAD taken a week of agonising uncertainty for Tara to make the decision to spend the weekend with Ryan, but once she'd made up her mind there was no looking back. It was for Pippa, she kept telling herself, not for her or Ryan. Although she had some trepidation at staying the night at Ryan's house, she felt reassured Christine would be there.

And Bethany? Tara hadn't seen her since the picnic, and wondered if their relationship had changed. She'd just have to wait and find out.

To her surprise, her parents hadn't shown as much resistance as she'd expected. She thought Ryan's ongoing care and surprising understanding of what it was like for a farmer to be out of action might have softened Graham's attitude. Her mother had been all for it after she'd grilled Ryan on the phone and convinced herself he was capable of looking after her precious daughter. She said Tara deserved a break away from the farm and the opportunity to experience something she really wanted to do.

She'd also assured her they could manage without her. The fact that Graham, now confident and much more mobile in his fibreglass walking cast, could do a few light chores made it easier.

The sun was low in the sky as Tara drove out of the clinic car park on Friday afternoon. Squinting against the harsh light, she took a right-hand turn towards Keysdale instead of her usual left to go home to the farm.

Her heart thudded with nerves but she wasn't about to change her mind. Going to the city to assist an orthopaedic surgeon with a major operation on one of her patients would have been routine for most doctors, but for Tara... She saw it as a turning point, a breaking away from the rigid routine of her life, and was grateful to the man who was about to make it happen.

Although she was staying with Ryan for two days, *and two nights*—she shivered at the thought—he'd promised to be the perfect host, in the role of a good friend only. He planned to take her out to dinner on Saturday night and Tara was looking forward to spending time with him.

As she pulled into the motel drive Ryan opened the front door of his unit. He must have been looking out for her. He walked down to meet her.

'Hi,' he said with a smile that set her heart dancing. 'I hope you're okay with me driving?'

'That's fine. I'm actually a bit weary. It's been a busy week.'

'For me too. I'm looking forward to an early night, so I hope you don't mind if we get some takeaway and maybe watch a DVD.'

'Sounds perfect.'

'That's if Bethany's settled for the night,' he added with a frown. 'Christine told me she's been hyped to the max today, so it's the luck of the draw whether she wears herself out or gets her second wind.' His frown deepened. 'But I guess we have to cross that bridge when we come to it.'

Tara couldn't help admiring Ryan for caring so much about his daughter's happiness and wellbeing. Despite his commitments he definitely wanted to be there for Bethany, no matter how much effort he had to put in.

He leaned into the car so she could grasp his neck while he lifted her out. He performed the task smoothly, as if he'd done it a thousand times before. Tara often resented the times when she had to relinquish her independence but today she felt comfortable and safe.

Too comfortable. Too safe!

She reminded herself she had vowed to keep a safe emotional distance from Ryan, but his physical closeness was getting in the way.

'Are you all right? You look a bit pale.'

He must have homed in on her uneasiness, but at least she wasn't blushing.

'I'm fine. As I said, it's been a long day.'

'Well, the sooner we get on the road, the better.'

Definitely—so she didn't have the opportunity to change her mind.

Tara's concerns about spending the evening with Ryan were unfounded. When they arrived at Ryan's apartment Beth was an over-excited dynamo.

After she gave Tara the grand tour of the apartment, which involved at least half an hour in the child's room examining every toy in her toybox, every item of clothing she possessed and all the other accoutrements that came with being a four-year-old girl going on fourteen, they had a quiet meal in the living room, watching Beth's favourite DVD.

'Time for bed,' Ryan announced at half past nine, which was at least two hours after her usual bedtime.

The noisy protest was as fierce as if he'd asked

her to spend the night in a dark, cold dungeon full of spiders.

'No!' she announced dramatically. 'I'm not tired.'

The argument went on for a good ten minutes until Beth finally conceded to go to bed only if Tara read her a bedtime story. After two stories, a request for a drink and dealing with a bladder that seemed to be as active as its owner, she finally settled. By that time Tara had little energy left for anything more than a soothing hot shower and a comfortable bed.

'I'm totally bushed,' Tara apologised.

'What would you like to do?' Ryan said, with a face that gave nothing away of what he was thinking.

'Have a shower and go to bed.'

She might have been mistaken, but she thought she noticed the slightest twinkle in Ryan's eyes. It didn't last long, though.

'I'll get Christine to help.'

Christine had a large bedroom, with space enough for a couple of comfy chairs, a small television and a desk. Ryan had arranged for her to share the second bathroom with Tara for the weekend, which was a much more sensible arrangement than using Ryan's *en-suite*.

'No. I'm sure I can manage. It's a huge shower recess, and I see you have support rails in all the right places.' Tara suspected Ryan had had the rails installed especially for her benefit, but she wasn't about to question him on it.

'Okay, just holler if you have any problems.'

'I doubt that I will.'

Their interaction was all very civilised—as if Ryan was putting up a mate for the weekend; as if nothing more intimate had happened in the past than an enduring platonic friendship.

And that suited Tara just fine.

She managed the shower without needing help, and had no trouble transferring to the double bed. Although it took her a while to get to sleep, when she finally did she slept soundly, and was woken by a soft knock on the door. She glanced at the clock. It was just after six but already the sun was streaming through her window.

'Come in,' she said sleepily as she rearranged her pyjama top and pulled the covers up to her chin. When the door opened her reaction to seeing Ryan in boxers and a crumpled tee shirt with a steaming cup in his hand took her by surprise.

The intimacy she'd tried so hard to avoid was standing in her doorway, with a grin on his face and an aura of good times past and possibilities for the future floating around him. If he'd come across and kissed her she wouldn't have been accountable for her actions.

But he didn't. He was playing the perfect gentleman.

'I'm afraid it will have to be cereal for breakfast. Christine and Beth are still asleep, and I wanted to get to the hospital in plenty of time for you to familiarise yourself with the set-up. Make sure you're comfortable with the equipment and the OR routine.' He cleared his throat and walked over to place the cup on her bedside table. 'Though I doubt much has changed over the past ten years or so.'

'Cereal's fine.' She wanted some time alone to make sense of the *rightness*—that was the best way she could describe her feelings—of having Ryan in her bedroom at just after dawn on a Saturday morning, when she'd normally be helping with the milking. But he seemed reluctant to leave. She positioned herself a little higher in the bed and leaned over to get the cup. 'And thanks for the tea.'

'My pleasure. Is there anything else I can get you or do for you?'

'No, thanks. I'll be fine. As soon as I've finished

this I'll get dressed and come through for breakfast.'

Ryan finally got the message and left her to the task of getting ready for a day working in the operating theatre, helping to give Pippa a better quality of life, working side by side with the man who had made it all possible.

She had every right to feel nervous and excited and happy all at the same time.

But she had no more time to ponder the unusual turn her life had taken. The door burst open and Bethany charged in like a rocket, all sparks and multi-colours and the joy of living that only the young were capable of exuding by the bucketload.

'I love you, Tara,' the little girl said as she flung her arms around Tara's neck and kissed her cheek. 'And I wish you could stay here all the time.'

'I love you too,' she whispered as a tear trickled down her cheek.

But any thoughts of the future with Ryan and his darling daughter were pure fantasy.

She lifted Bethany off the bed gently.

'I need to get dressed now, so why don't you help your daddy make some breakfast?'

'Ooh, yes.' Tara could almost see the cogs of

Beth's young brain turning as she catapulted out of the room with almost as much energy as she'd entered.

Pippa's surgery, though complicated, went smoothly. The operation took just over three hours, but at the conclusion there was an air in the OR of a job well done, thanks to the surgical team and especially to Tara.

She'd been amazing. From the time she'd appeared in her dark blue scrubs to the moment she'd stripped off her gloves and gown and wheeled out of the theatre there'd been an incredibly positive buzz in the air.

Ryan touched her shoulder and she swung around.

'Thanks, Tara. You were great. Amazing, in fact.' He smiled and swung open the heavy theatre door.

'I should be thanking you. You're the one who went to so much trouble to organise it all,' she said as she manoeuvred through the opening. 'It went well?'

'Better than I expected. I am hopeful Pippa's new hip will last for at least twenty years.'

'And then? She'll still be a relatively young woman.' The joy in Tara's eyes dimmed for a moment.

'Unfortunately I can't predict that far ahead, but we'll just have to cross that bridge when we come to it.' Ryan stopped outside the recovery ward. 'I just want to see if Pippa's awake and tell her the good news. Then I can meet you in the staff lounge.'

'Do you want me to talk to her parents? They'll be desperate to know how things went.'

'I was going to do that after checking on Pippa—maybe we can go together.'

Tara nodded. 'I'd like that.' She hesitated a moment. 'And can I come in with you now?'

'Of course.' Ryan opened the door.

Pippa was one of two post-op patients in a room that was usually a hubbub of activity during the week. Although there were usually one or two surgeons who did elective sessions on Saturday morning, the theatres were geared mainly for emergencies on the weekend.

A nurse stood on the side of the bed, writing down her patient's obs, and the anaesthetist was at its head, monitoring the girl's breathing. They both looked up and acknowledged Ryan and Tara's presence as they entered the room. Pippa's endotracheal tube was still in place, but she was breathing spontaneously and beginning to cough, a sure sign the tube was ready to come out.

'You two did excellent work today.' The anaesthetist looked up briefly before focusing his attention on the task of removing the tube and replacing it with an oxygen mask. 'Is this going to be a regular thing? Your assistant would certainly be an asset here.'

Ryan glanced at Tara, whose cheeks had taken on a rosy pink colour. She certainly deserved the praise and had no reason to be embarrassed.

'No, I'm afraid this is a one-off,' Tara said huskily. She paused to clear her throat. 'I live and work three hours' drive away. Ryan went to the trouble of setting all this up because Pippa's a very special patient of mine.'

The anaesthetist glanced at her and smiled. 'Well, if you ever change your mind…'

Just then Pippa produced a loud gurgling cough and opened her eyes.

'You're in the recovery ward,' the nurse said, a tad louder than was necessary. 'And your wonderful doctors are here to tell you how the surgery went.'

Pippa closed her eyes briefly, before opening them again and turning her head slightly so she could see both Tara and Ryan.

'Do you want to tell her the good news?' Ryan asked softly.

Tara nodded and smiled as she positioned herself as close as she could to the bed. She reached out to grasp the young woman's hand and felt the slightest squeeze.

'It all went really well, Pippa. It will take a couple of days, but Dr Dennison tells me you'll be up and running soon.'

Ryan leaned a little closer. 'And I'll be in to see you tomorrow.'

Pippa managed the slightest smile and then closed her drowsy eyes again, signalling she'd absorbed all the information she could for the moment.

They both quietly left, and Ryan was suddenly overwhelmed by a sense of shared accomplishment, a special bond with Tara that went deeper than any professional relationship ever could.

He needed to talk to her—without the distraction of his over-exuberant daughter.

And he would do it over dinner tonight.

Ryan had informed Tara he'd booked a meal at one of his favourite restaurants, renowned for its superb food and casual atmosphere. And it was within walking distance of his apartment.

'They won't turn you away if you're wearing jeans, but I guess you'd call the dress code "smart casual",' Ryan had told her the previous week, when they'd been making the final arrangements for the weekend.

Knowing she didn't need to dress in a designer outfit was a relief, and she felt satisfied as she looked in the mirror after putting on her make-up and scooping her hair up from her neck and fixing it with a gold clasp. She certainly wouldn't win a beauty contest, she thought as she retouched her blusher and removed a speck of errant mascara, but she scrubbed up okay if you didn't look too closely at her from the waist down.

She rarely had the opportunity to go out, let alone to a city restaurant with a dangerously handsome man she was beginning to care about more than she'd planned. She kept telling herself she was looking forward to the outing, but there was a persistent niggle of anxiety in her gut she just couldn't seem to shift.

Her weekend with Ryan seemed too perfect—being fussed over by both Ryan and Christine; all the compliments on the good work she'd done in the operating theatre; being wined and dined by an attractive man; having the opportunity to spend some quality time with a delightful four-year-old who seemed to adore her. She had the ominous feeling it was all too good to be true. The reality was when Ryan dropped her home the following evening nothing would have changed. But she could see no alternative, and resolved not to let her ruminations interfere with her evening.

As she wheeled herself out of the bedroom and along the short passage to the informal living area she could hear the sounds of Christine in the kitchen, no doubt busy preparing a meal for herself and her young charge. Ryan sat with his daughter on his knee, watching television. They both looked up when they heard the bump of her chair as she stopped and put on the brakes.

Ryan's eyes were as wide as his daughter's.

'You look like a bootiful princess,' Bethany said with her usual candour.

'And I second that.' Ryan gently moved his daughter and stood up. He wore charcoal pants, a plain navy shirt and a china-blue silk tie. He looked gorgeous. He grabbed his jacket from the back of the chair and slipped it on before planting a kiss on Tara's cheek. 'In fact you look stunning,' he added as he ran the tip of his tongue along his bottom lip.

'Thank you. And you scrub up pretty well yourself.'

It was Tara's way of making light of the compliment and it apparently worked. Ryan chuckled.

'Are you ready to go, then?'

'Sure am.'

After hugs from Bethany, and a farewell wink from Christine, they set off. The restaurant was two blocks away, on the same street as Ryan's apartment, and when they arrived the place was buzzing. Ryan was on first-name terms with the head waiter and they were guided to a table in a corner with plenty of space for Tara's chair.

'Well, at least you don't have to worry about pulling out my chair,' Tara teased.

Ryan smiled without answering as he handed her the wine list.

'What would you like to drink?' he finally said.

'Just water to start, and maybe some wine with dinner. Unlike you, I have to *drive* home, and I don't want to be picked up for being out of control on a public footpath.'

He laughed as he poured chilled water into a crystal tumbler.

When the wine waiter appeared Tara didn't hear what Ryan said to him, but he came back in a few minutes with a long-necked bottle of a local boutique beer.

'I hope you don't mind?'

'No, of course not.'

Tara couldn't help noticing Ryan wasn't fully at ease. There was something on his mind. Something that was probably none of her business but that made her feel a little edgy as well.

'Is something the matter?' Tara wanted to clear the air.

Ryan paused and cleared his throat.

'Part of the reason I asked you out to dinner was that I wanted to talk to you. Over the past month you've been treating me like a leper, and we've not had a chance to talk through what's happening with us since I've been in Keysdale.' He traced lines in the condensation on his glass and then looked up with an expression that went right to the centre of Tara's heart.

'I…er…don't understand what you mean,' Tara said with her heart thudding.

'We need to talk about the accident. We were both so young, and I didn't want to hurt you and go against what you told me you really wanted, but I know now that walking out on you was the wrong thing. I should have tried harder to convince you we could survive, no matter what. I also believe you weren't telling me the truth when you said you didn't love me. I think it was just your way of ending a relationship you believed had no future.'

Ryan looked down at his drink and took a slow sip.

Tara was close to tears.

'No. Don't blame yourself. If anyone's to blame it's me. I wasn't thinking straight and I felt sorry for myself. I could only see a future abounding with problems. I knew you felt really bad about the accident, and I didn't want to fuel your guilt by having you living with me as a daily reminder of what happened. I shouldn't have sent you away, and I was kidding myself by thinking the love had gone for me.' She reached out for Ryan's hand and gave it a squeeze. 'I've always loved you and I always will.' Her voice dropped to whisper. 'And I'm sorry for the damage I've done to our relationship. I wish there was some way—'

'Maybe there is.' Ryan's eyes were bright with hope and anticipation. 'It's something I've thought a lot about over the last few weeks and I hoped I could tell you tonight.'

Tara raised her eyebrows and waited, wondering what he was about to say.

He grasped her hand with both of his, adoration shining from his eyes.

'I want to move to Keysdale.'

'But—'

'No, hear me out. It wouldn't happen overnight, but I'm sure I could secure a consultancy in Bayfield—and Rob Whelan has offered me more sessions already. It's a wonderful place for Bethany to grow up in. We could build a house together, work together. Have babies together.'

Tara was overwhelmed, but she had no doubt in her mind that Ryan was serious.

'What exactly are you saying, Ryan?' Her grip on his hand tightened.

'My darling Tara, I want a second chance. I want us to be married again.' He paused. 'And I'm certain it could work for all of us, as the family we always wanted to be.'

Tara didn't know what to say. Ryan was offering her the future she'd always dreamed of and she couldn't think of a single reason not to accept his proposal.

'Well?' he said with a grin on his face.

'Yes, Ryan. Of course I'll marry you.'

Right on cue the waiter arrived with two frosted flutes and a bottle of vintage champagne.

'How did you do that?'

He laughed, leaned across and planted a lingering kiss on her lips.

'That's my secret.'

EPILOGUE

Two and a half years later.

IT TOOK six months to build the house but, like everything else in Ryan's plans, he'd wanted it to be perfect. It had all the features to make life easy for a wheelchair-user, her husband, her stepdaughter and their new baby—and as many children as they wanted. It even had a self-contained unit for Christine under the same roof.

The rambling single-storey country home stood proudly in ten gently rolling, lightly wooded acres in the foothills about ten kilometres east of Keysdale. There was a small paddock that was home to a gentle rust-coloured Shetland pony named Missy, an orchard of a dozen young fruit trees, and a well-tended herb garden. Today, being a very special day, a little six-year-old girl sat quietly on the veranda, gently rocking a cradle, waiting for her grandparents to arrive.

The girl looked around and smiled as the front door opened.

'I'll look after Brodie while you go and get changed,' Tara said, as Beth ran over to plant her trademark sloppy kiss on Tara's cheek.

'You look beautiful.' Bethany's smile broadened into a grin.

'Why, thank you.' She wheeled herself over to her four-month-old baby, who was sleeping peacefully. 'Your daddy just told me the same, so I guess it must be true.' She laughed as she gently ran her index finger over the baby's forehead.

She was talking to herself as Beth had already run inside.

Her mind began to wander as she settled into the rhythm of gently swinging her darling sleeping son.

So much had happened since Ryan had asked her to be his wife and the mother of his children. Her initial reaction had been one of incredulity. She'd half believed Ryan had lost touch with reality when he'd outlined his plans for their life together. He'd managed to counter every objection she'd made, though, with ideas that were not only rational and well thought out but *possible*. He'd turned what she'd thought was an impossible dream into the reality of the 'happily ever after' life she was living right now.

'Who would care for Bethany?'

'Christine's prepared to work for us for as long as we want her.'

'You want more kids. I can't—'

'Why not?'

And the living breathing evidence was lying in the cradle in front of her.

'My work?' By that time her protests had lost a little of their clout.

'If we're going to set up house in Keysdale there's no need to change anything—unless you want to. I've already approached the boards of both the Keysdale and Bayfield hospitals and they're open to the idea of setting up an operating theatre so you can assist. My guess is that you'll have other surgeons clamouring for your services.'

She now worked two days in the clinic, as well as two sessions a week in the OR. She'd also recently embarked on part-time post-graduate studies in anaesthetics and hoped to add Diploma of Anaesthetics to her list of qualifications two years down the track.

At that moment Tara's thoughts were interrupted by a six-year-old dynamo dressed in a frothy pink dress and an aura of excitement. She burst through the front door, closely followed by her father.

'I heard a car coming. Is it Nan and Gramps?' the child said breathlessly as a vehicle pulled up in front of the house.

The baby stirred and Tara lifted him into her arms as Jane and Graham Fielding climbed out of the newly acquired four-wheel-drive they'd bought to tow their state-of-the-art caravan around Australia. Selling the farm seemed to have been one of the best things they'd done in their lives.

Jane barely stopped to hug Bethany and say hello to the adults before she had her grandson in her arms. Graham stood behind them and extended his hand.

'It's a beautiful day for a naming ceremony,' Graham said. 'Let's hope there are one or two more little ones to come.'

Tara glanced at her husband, aware of the flush of heat in her cheeks.

Ryan winked, moved over to where she sat and kissed her.

'I don't see any reason why not,' Ryan said.

* * * * *

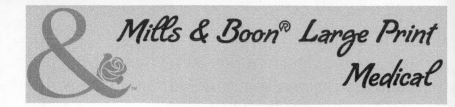

December

January

February

Mills & Boon® Large Print Medical

March

April

May